About the Author

L.A. Detwiler is an author and high school English teacher from Hollidaysburg, Pennsylvania. During her final year at Mount Aloysius College, she started writing her first fiction novel, which was published in 2015. She has also written articles that have appeared in several women's publications and websites. L.A. Detwiler lives in her hometown with her husband, Chad. They have five cats and a mastiff named Henry.

THE WIDOW NEXT DOOR

L. A. Detwiler

Published by AVON
A division of HarperCollins*Publishers* Ltd
1 London Bridge Street
London SE1 9GF

www.harpercollins.co.uk

This paperback edition 2019

First published in Great Britain by HarperCollins*Publishers* 2018

A catalogue copy of this book is available from the British Library.

ISBN: 978-0-00-832464-3

This novel is entirely a work of fiction. The names, characters
and incidents portrayed in it are the work of the author's imagination.
Any resemblance to actual persons, living or dead,
events or localities is entirely coincidental.

Typeset in Birka by Palimpsest Book Production Limited,
Falkirk, Stirlingshire
Printed and bound in UK by CPI Group (UK) Ltd,
Croydon CR0 4YY

MIX
Paper from
responsible sources
FSC™ C007454

This book is produced from independently certified FSC™ paper
to ensure responsible forest management.

For more information visit: www.harpercollins.co.uk/green

To my husband, Chad.

'There are some secrets which do not permit themselves
to be told.'

– Edgar Allan Poe

Prologue

Looking back, there were warning signs. Flickers of who she was hiding, what *they* were hiding. I just didn't want to see. Maybe I didn't want the fantasy world I'd created to disappear. Maybe I wanted to keep believing their love story was perfect, would be my comfortable company for my final years. Maybe I hoped it would remind me of my own early love story, of that swooning feeling, of those first-kiss moments. Maybe I just missed him, and I was soothing that pain by watching them.

Whatever it was, I know this – things are changing now. *They're* changing.

They're breaking.

I think it started as tiny cracks, almost unnoticeable signals of them coming undone. The angry gesture on the front porch over some argument I couldn't hear, smoothed by a kiss on the cheek and what looked like an apology. Abandoned dinner one night in the kitchen, a screaming match ensuing as she stormed out ... followed by a sweet, tender embrace at breakfast the next morning.

I thought they were running their course, fighting like couples do. I thought maybe the honeymoon years were just wearing off because we all know they *do* wear off.

I thought they were okay. Maybe they thought that too.

But as the weeks go on, I realise something I hadn't before. Something's not right. Something's not right at all. In fact, something's so grotesquely wrong and hideously tainted, I don't know if there will be any turning back.

Things haven't been right for a while now, I'm starting to realise. Behind that bubbly smile, that sunshine yellow, she's not perfect. Not even close.

Why with all bright stories is there a monster, unseen, that festers beneath the boiling surface?

As the weather gets colder, the frost settling in, it's clear that maybe I didn't really know my neighbour from 312 Bristol Lane at all.

Chapter 1

They moved in to 312 Bristol Lane on a Thursday, a blazing July sun gleaming off the white picket fence as if everything was about to change. I stared on as Amos sat purring on my lap, cuddled against the afghan covering my legs. I stroked his angora-like fur, watching box after box spew into the house. Their smiles were palpable across the yard, my view unobstructed by blinds, draperies or annoying trees. I could see it all, every smile, every box, every hope going into that two-storey. Aside from the newcomers, the always deserted road remained that way, and I was glad. For the first time in a long time, I was thankful I lived on a dead-end street, the only people on the cul-de-sac me and 312 Bristol Lane. It gave me a chance to watch without obstruction or distraction. I smiled, Amos's purrs calming me.

I was glad to have neighbours again. The months that 312 Bristol Lane sat empty were truly boring. It had been a while since there was life next door, the real estate sign sitting in the front lawn for longer than it ever had over the years. Maybe the house was just waiting for the right people to buy it, or maybe the market was on a downward spiral. Whatever was happening, I missed having activity on the lane, having someone to watch and to learn about.

I could tell from that first day that this new couple would be exciting to study, unlike the last neighbours who had left in quite a hurry. It had been a while since I had someone next door who truly interested me. There have been several couples over the many years I've lived here, but even on that first day, I knew there was something different about these two people. They felt different than all the couples who had lived there before.

From the first day I saw them, the couple was, quite simply, mesmerising. I think it was just the way they interacted with each other. It was electric, and I liked them right away. I found it comforting to watch the young couple, so obviously in love. You *had* to be in love to be skipping under the stifling heat, carrying box after box until your arms felt like they would fall off. I've been through only a few moves in my lifetime, but it's enough to know moving isn't particularly fun. Still, the lively young couple jaunted up the steps, leaning to help each other out. The woman, a perky blonde, seemed especially excited, dancing around the front lawn, eyeing up their new dream home, calling the man who was clearly her husband over to peer at a discovered flower or a charming feature.

I pulled the afghan tighter around my legs, feeling simultaneously happy for the couple and a little envious. I would give anything to be her, wearing a sundress on a day like that. Instead, my old body shivered despite the heat. Getting old meant the loss of so much, and warmth was no exception.

The blonde-haired woman stooped down to stow a box on the front step, and the black-haired man followed suit. He wore a simple grey shirt and some pants, nothing fancy. I couldn't fault him for that. It was move-in day, after all. Fashion could take a back seat on a day like that.

The blonde wrapped her arms around her man, his arms currently empty. The two embraced on the front step of their brand-new home, a sparkling new life ahead of them. They kissed, and I felt my cheeks moving into a smile at the sight. It was beautiful to see young love again, to remember that feeling, to recall the burning desire I'd once felt in my own youth when I'd been a perky blonde who wore short sleeves instead of afghans on a July day.

In some ways, I could feel the warmth flooding my veins, could feel my own husband's kiss on my lips, like it had just happened. In other ways, sitting in the stiff rocking chair, staring out the window, it felt like a lifetime ago. My aching hands stroking Amos's soft fur, I leaned my head back, rocking gently, taking in the sight as the young couple smooched.

I got up a few times that day, stirring Amos from his sleep, to get a cup of tea, to use the bathroom, to wander to the sofa to watch my soap operas on the television at noon. For most of the day, though, I sat, rocking aimlessly, blissfully watching the ins and outs of the new couple.

Their smiles enlivened me. Their joyous skipping, despite their clear exhaustion, energised me. I sat for a long time just wondering how their story would unfold, feeling lucky to be privy to their interactions. I would get to uncover their lives from right here. I would get to be a witness to their love.

The thought thrilled me. After so much loneliness, I had something to look forward to. My heart swelled.

This was what love looked like, love in its truest, purest form, love ready to take on life.

Staring out that window on that summer day, though, I hoped the couple could make it last, could hang on to the kiss on the front steps.

Despite my silent prayers, I knew without a doubt that, before long, the joy would fade and the couple's dream home would become a slaughterhouse not much unlike my own.

A woman has a way of knowing these things.

Chapter 2

My bones are creaking, a pain working its way from the inside out. It's such a chore sometimes to even get moving, to walk across the kitchen, to stoop down to feed Amos. Some days, it's a hardship to even prod myself out of bed, the comforter enveloping me in a way that says 'stay'.

Sometimes, I think about staying in bed all day, my scratchy, aged blanket wrapped around me like a cocoon, protecting me from the vile world. There are worse things than to perish tucked in a warm bed, worn-out blanket or not.

Nevertheless, I deny myself the luxury of oblivion the bed offers. Instead, I wander over to Amos's food station, the sweet cat already meowing, awaiting his morsels of food. I carefully open the can, scraping some of the gloppy tuna-like concoction onto his plate before making my own tea. It's silly, I know, serving a cat before myself. But Amos is my best friend, my everything. It makes me feel good to have someone to pamper, to care for. It feels good to be needed.

After getting my cup of tea, only filled halfway, of course – I've learned the perils of a full cup the hard way – I trudge over to my spot, the familiar wood of the rocking chair welcoming me back into position. I rock for a moment, gently appraising the day, as is my custom. The sun is just coming up, glinting off the newly fallen leaves of reds, golds and oranges. It's my favourite scene out my window, the cool breeze of the autumn air gently lifting the edges of the decayed leaves. Even in here, with the dusty smell of an ageing house, I can close my eyes and smell the earthy scent of autumn, feel the brisk air on my face, and see his perfect smile.

He always loved this time of year. In our younger days, he would drag me pumpkin picking at the Johnsons' farm, hay bales lined up to lead the way. I'd roll my eyes and tell him it was pointless. Deep down, though, I loved those afternoons, wandering on the farm, choosing the right pumpkin we'd carve up that night accompanied by hot apple cider. I wish, even now, I could tell him I loved those days.

I should've told him how much I loved those days.

I sigh, my eyes temporarily averted by the sight of the neighbour – Alexander Clarke. He's off to work, bright and early, before the day has really begun. He straightens his tie, a hand running through his hair, before jumping into his automobile and heading down the road.

It's been three months since he and Jane moved in, three months of joyful furniture buying and evenings on their porch and walks. Three months of front-porch kisses and squealing laughter in the front yard. Three months of sheer happiness, of love in its truest, purest form.

At first, I'd worried they'd think it odd, an old woman and her cat peering out at them. I hesitated some mornings, wondering if I *was* being creepy, staring into the lives, into the business of others so regularly.

But I couldn't peel myself away.

It became something to look forward to, studying them,

watching them, trying to piece together their story from what I can see. It's quite a fun game, really, and I get to learn more than one would think. From driveway goodbyes to outdoor chores, I can judge a lot about them, can put together so many titbits into a clear puzzle of my design. What's more, they haven't put up a blind in the window of their dining room or even draperies. The large bay window sits unobstructed by anything, its sparkling clear glass giving me a full view of their heavy wooden table. I get to be privy to their mealtimes, to their interactions, to their morning coffee.

I know. It seems ridiculous. But I can't, I just *can't*, take myself away from them. There's something haunting about young love, about getting to see it all unfold. And for an old lady like me, alone and bored, these stories, these interactions, they keep me going. They make that creaky exit out of bed a little more bearable. They give me something intriguing to wrap myself up in.

I've come to learn that it's okay, anyway. They're so engrossed with each other, in their lives, they don't notice a frail old woman peering out her window at them. Mornings when he leaves for work, afternoons when she busies herself with household work or other tasks, or evenings when they're together, they've always got something to keep themselves go, go, going. The life of the young is exhaustingly busy.

Not that they're stuck-up or selfish. No, they're neighbourly enough. Well, at least the woman is. She came over about three days after they moved in, knocked on my door around eleven in the morning.

Let's be clear: I liked Jane from the day she moved in. The way she carried herself, the way she ambled around even when she was clearly exhausted from moving – I saw something there. And once she came over for the first time, I really liked her, a deep-seated, internal liking of her.

Still, brewing beneath the surface, I felt something else, too. Maybe it was just paranoia roiling from my lonely days, or maybe I've just spent too much time in my own head. But something in me flopped when she came over, something unsettling finding its way to the surface. Not enough to make me change my mind about her – but enough to damage the perfect view of her just a little bit, just enough to make me slightly uncomfortable.

Nonetheless, there was something about her from day one that made that nervous anxiety easy to ignore, even if I shouldn't have.

* * *

It was quite the task to hobble to the door before she scurried away, thinking me asleep. I rushed into the hallway, reminding myself to be careful, that it wouldn't do to fall and hurt myself. How sad are the days when a broken hip becomes one's biggest fear?

I made it in time, the girl standing in a bright yellow sundress holding a pie. Yellow is her colour. It makes her blonde hair look even blonder. It fits her complexion nicely. It fits with her neon personality. Maybe I'm partial, though. I've always been fond of yellow since I was a little girl. It's a happy colour.

'Hi, nice to meet you! I'm the new neighbour: Jane Clarke. I just thought since you're our only neighbour, I'd stop and say hi.'

I smiled, her energy contagious. She was bubbling and talking a mile a minute, the youth and naivety about life softening her in ways I was no longer soft. Looking into her clear blue eyes, I saw such hope and such dreams.

I missed those days.

'That's so nice, dear. Yes, it's great to talk to you. How is your move going?'

'Wonderful, thanks for asking. I just love this street. So quiet and peaceful. No traffic, no noise with the dead end and all. And how lucky, we have such a big lot, huh! And all of the peace, the privacy. I just love it here. I knew from the second I saw this house we had to have it. My husband Alex wasn't so sure about it, but once I saw it, the deal was sealed.'

'Yes. Bristol Lane is a quiet street. Kind of lonely sometimes, but overall, I like the peace. And your house is gorgeous.'

'Oh, silly me. I'm sure you're probably busy. But here's a pie I made for you. I hope you like rhubarb. My husband says no one likes rhubarb pie, but I beg to differ.'

My hands literally clapped together. 'Oh my, that's my favourite. These old hands are too tired to bake many pies these days. Thank you. This is so lovely. Will you come in for tea?' I shakily took the pie from her, revelling in the perfect golden crust. It had been so long since I'd had a rhubarb pie. I could hardly believe my good fortune. I didn't even think anyone made rhubarb pie these days. It was like a blast from the past calling me home, and I didn't hesitate to take up the offer.

I knew the girl was special from the first day she moved in. There was no denying it.

Of course, she's not a girl. She's a woman. Still, at my age, everyone under seventy seems like a girl. Age is all about perspective, and mine's become quite a distant perspective these days.

'Oh, I couldn't possibly. My husband's at work today, and I have some cleaning to get done. But definitely soon, okay?'

11

'Yes, dear. That would be great. Stop back anytime. Congratulations,' I said, and Jane was gone, her lean legs carrying her down my porch steps and across the yard to her house, the skip in her step matching her bubbly personality.

I smiled, feeling I now had the best neighbours in the world, even if she did rush off pretty quickly. It was so thoughtful of her to bring by a pie, to spend time with an old woman like me, even if it was just a few minutes. I wished for a moment she would've stayed longer, but I didn't want to cause trouble, not on our first meeting. So I let it go, thinking about how great it would be to have someone to talk to, wondering why I'd gotten goose bumps at the sight of her walking away.

*   *   *

As often happens, life for the young gets overrun by daily routines and to-do lists and the pressing matters of youth. She hasn't been back since that first day. The rhubarb pie is long gone, and it saddens me a little bit. I had high hopes for us back then. I'd imagined all of the conversations, the lunches, the teas we'd share. I'd imagined what it would be like after all these years to have, dare I hope, a friend of sorts. But dreams don't always go as planned, do they? And sometimes our biggest hopes are shattered by reality.

In truth, 312 Bristol Lane hasn't quite turned out like I'd imagined at all. There has been little interaction for the past few months except for a few small encounters – and arguably, even they were a bit off-kilter.

On Sunday, I was making my glorious trek in my good old station wagon to Mark's Mart for a few supplies. Jane had been cleaning the windows outside the house, and she gazed at the street from the top of her ladder. I smiled and tooted the horn. She didn't wave, staring as if in another world.

I suppose she'd just been busy. That had to be it.

Regardless, there have been no visits, no more pies. I tell myself I can't be annoyed, though. Life at that age is blissfully full. There will be plenty of time for tea drinking and porch sitting with elderly ladies and other generally dull tasks. Right now, she's got other priorities.

I do worry. There've been subtle changes, small happenings, that have caused that nervous anxiety to resurge. Mostly, the anxiety is for them, the couple at 312 Bristol Lane.

Fewer goodbye kisses on the porch step, less hand holding at breakfast. I'm sure I'm overanalysing. It's not enough to worry just yet. It's a subtle change – but a change nonetheless.

Then again, maybe it's all me. Maybe I'm imagining it. Perhaps these are just the musings of an overly bored woman. It's no secret that I've got way too much time on my hands. Perhaps I need to find a hobby – but what? Knitting always did seem quite monotonous. Besides, these bones are too achy, too rickety, to be of any real use. And who would I knit for? Amos? I doubt the white Persian would want anything to do with a scratchy, crooked sweater I'd put together.

Besides, it's much more fun watching. I've become quite a good observer in my late age.

It's not all bad, either. Jane at 312 Bristol Lane still seems happy. She still smiles, skips around the house in a chipper fashion, saunters to the mailbox in her gorgeous sundresses, kicks back her feet as she leans on the front porch step.

To most, she probably looks the same. To her husband, she probably looks the same.

To me, though, I can see it, the shifting, the small clues

that not all is well. Like a detective in waiting, I sit, pondering over the signs, wondering how they all fit together in the bigger picture that is her.

The only question is: what can I do about it? What can this old lady in her rocking chair who can barely walk the twenty feet to the bathroom in time do about it?

For now, all I can do is keep watching, keep waiting, and keep hoping she'll come over. In truth, it would be good to feel a little needed.

Chapter 3

It's Saturday, and they're raking leaves together. It looks warm out, the picture-perfect day you see on cards or those made-for-television movies that make me seriously want to crawl outside of my skin.

Not that love is a bad thing. But those movies where every-thing is perfect, the woman swooning over a dozen roses like some sickeningly debilitated puppet — those are the things that make me roll my eyes and shake my head, even when there's nothing else on. Maybe it's just me, though. Maybe I've just got a deeper understanding of life and love than most, especially the not-so-rosy moments. Maybe if life were a little bit more like a made-for-television movie, things wouldn't be such a wreck right now. Sometimes predictability makes life happy.

I digress, though. Because the point is, 312 Bristol Lane doesn't look like one of those annoyingly sappy movies. The couple feels real to me. They feel genuine, even in the happy moments. I don't begrudge them these moments.

Jane and Alex keep raking leaves, right through my exis-tential crisis over sappy movies and predictable plots. I refocus, studying them, looking at their subtle cues as I rock, Amos in my lap.

15

Alex has got short sleeves on, the rake in his hand. Jane's in a lightweight sweater, her hair up in a ponytail. She's sitting on the steps, chatting away animatedly. I sort of want to open the window, to get some air and to hear what they're talking about, but I think it would be a little obvious. Plus, I'd probably just get cold in a minute or two, and I don't want to disturb Amos. He's all cosy, purring gently. His feet are even moving as he dreams.

The pile of leaves is getting bigger and bigger. Alex's back is to me, but I can tell by his posture he's relaxed, despite the work. She's talking away. She talks with her hands. Did I used to be a hand talker when I had the energy? When I had someone to talk to?

I can't remember. So many things I can't remember now, it makes me feel sad. How do those moments slip away? The little moments, the little details, are like fleeting feathers on the breeze. I so desperately try to cling to them, if for no other reason than to say I can, but in truth, I can't. Time stomps forward, leaving our memories in the ashy dirt. We can't hold on to everything, not all of the big things and especially not the little things. Sometimes the loss of the little things hurts worse.

Now don't go feeling sorry for yourself, you old coot, I think to myself. *No need to get all down in the dumps. It won't change anything anyway. You've got plenty to be thankful for.*

Still, the quietude of the house can wear on a person. Talking to Amos just isn't the same. He's lovely, don't get me wrong. But he doesn't talk back. Sometimes the silence in the house is deafening. It's enough to make me want to scream ... but who would hear it?

The pointlessness is sometimes the difficulty of ageing,

16

especially when you're alone. No cat can fill that void or tackle that internal dilemma.

I've got other forms of social interaction, of course. I go to church on Sunday mornings when I feel up to it and when it isn't bad weather. These eyes don't work very well in the rain or when it's foggy, after all. Still, I step into the little church down the road now and again, sitting in the back pew where I used to sit at the stage in my life I needed God or something to soothe the internal wounds festering, bubbling and oozing. In truth, if I look hard, they're still there. I guess that's why I still go to Mass once in a while, when I can. The fire and brimstone speeches are extreme, but who am I to say what's right or wrong?

They also send a little shiver down my spine, all the talk about eternal damnation and forgiveness. I fiddle with my fingers during these sermons, asking the question so many do but so few truly understand: Will I be saved? Forgiven? Will I make it to heaven, or will my shattered soul spend eternity paying for my sins?

After all this time, I still don't know the answer. Maybe I don't want to know the answer, in truth. I don't know if a few Sunday Masses now and then can check off a box, can mitigate my wrongdoings. But it can't hurt.

Plus, if nothing else, Sundays get me out of this tomb of a house, out of the interminable chill of being alone.

After Mass, I say hello to a few of the ladies and even go downstairs for coffee once in a while. They don't really know me, which is okay. I'd probably forget their names anyway. I'm fine with being on the edges.

I also have my trips to the grocery store, Mark's Mart. There's a nice boy there who not only rings up my purchases but also loads my grocery bags in the car. He's a young fellow, too young really to be talking to an old lady like me. His smile, his kind words, they give me something to look forward to. Best of all, he knows exactly how the groceries need to be packed – chicken in its own bag, toiletries in a brown bag, Amos's cat food in a plastic bag. I have my system, and he doesn't mess with it. I respect that.

I've come to learn, though, it's the small, ordinary interactions you miss most when you're alone. The silence of the house at any given moment, the only sound my breathing. The fact there's no one to tell about the hilarious crisp commercial you just saw or to call out to when an adorable squirrel is eating on the feeder. The seemingly unimportant times, the little joys of daily life are lost when you don't have anyone to share them with.

Nevertheless, I promised myself years ago I wouldn't let that appreciation disappear. I vowed I'd cling to the positives. That's what he'd want, after all. That's what I need to do.

No matter how much I swear to myself I'll keep living, keep being thankful, it's not easy. I'd be lying if I said it was. It's not just the silence; it's the lack of companionship that makes me crazy.

It's him. It's the fact he's not here.

I miss him. In spite of everything, I know deep down we were soulmates. How could I *not* miss him?

I miss our breakfasts of pancakes on Sundays when he would talk about the shocking news stories in the paper. I miss his kisses, miss the way he would wrap an arm around me as he passed by. I miss our Saturday morning drives to nowhere in particular. I miss our movie marathons on the sofa, our apple sauce with mini marshmallows on top just for fun. I miss having someone to bake for, someone to share everything with. I miss the way he didn't give up on me even when I was falling apart, how his shoulder was there even when I didn't realise I wanted or needed it.

It's true, there was a time in our marriage when things weren't good. There was a large span of time when I didn't appreciate what we had. There were a lot of missed moments because I was – well, who I am.

I can't apologise for that. But I can apologise for not understanding what I had to lose. And it turns out, I had a lot to lose. The barren rooms surrounding me underscore this fact. I lost in the end, lost so much, and now I'm here, sweltering in the realisation that I didn't win.

I couldn't win, after all.

But before all the bad times, there *were* good times too. There were the moments when we first met, the moments of happiness. I know now there were beautiful times. I can see them now. I wish I'd seen them more clearly then. I wonder if he saw them for what they were, right up to the end. I wonder if he appreciated them, even when it was his time to go.

We were happy once. It's been so long, it's easy to forget that we *were* happy.

I think about that now, the good times, the quietness stirring feelings of regret. It is not the regret of him being gone that bothers me as much as the regret of lost time. Such is the plight of humanity, I guess. We don't realise what's important until it's way too late, until the time has evaporated. Then, when we have time to appreciate what matters most, we're alone, incapable of making up for those moments from our youth.

'That's enough,' I announce aloud to snap myself out of my sadness. I decided years ago that attitude is a choice. I try not to let myself sulk for too long. Once you start sulking, you're done for. What good will that do? There's no denying that what happened plagues me, haunts me, ravages me. But I have to maintain some semblance of existence, which means I have to cling to the positives.

I have to. There's no choice.

And right now, 312 Bristol Lane is helping me ignore – or maybe avoid – the past. Their love story is helping me see what could be, what's left.

I return my attention to them. They're still raking leaves, the pile sky-high now. She's laughing, stretching out her long legs in the sunshine, leaning back with her face towards the great blue, contentedness radiating from her soft grin.

This is what Saturday mornings should be about.

I smile as I watch him, clearly feeling mischievous, kick up a pile of leaves at her. The dirty, dingy leaves fall onto her, clinging on to her clothes. One even lands in her hair. She screams, a shriek of irritation and glee simultaneously. It's so loud, I can hear remnants of it through the window. I tap my fingers on my rocking chair, completely enthralled as she leaps to her feet and races after him, poking him, tickling him, even hitting at him as he laughs. He dashes through their front yard and a chase around the property ensues. They run like children on the first day of summer break, her laughter still heard as he begs her to stop.

After a few laps, they are both panting. He pauses, leaning on his knees, out of breath. A once-familiar warmth surges within me from witnessing their connection, a love I can sense from over here.

A beautiful love.

Then, in the front yard, right on the lawn, he pulls her in to him, smack against his chest. They kiss, a sweet kiss turning passionate. He pulls her tighter, and she rests her chin on his shoulder. They sway a little, and eventually he pulls back, twirling her as they dance in the pile of leaves.

It's a magical moment, a moment way better than my television movies. It's a real moment.

They stand for a while in the leaves until the moment fades. Then, he saunters to the garage for the leaf bags, and she stands, wrapping her arms around herself, smiling at nothing but the feelings left behind.

It's my favourite moment since they've moved in. It's an everyday kind of moment, but it's the sort of moment that I'd give anything to have again.

I sit watching them swirl in joy, a pure kind of joy, as he returns with the leaf bag. They swoop down, scooping up leaves together, laughing despite the chore at hand. She playfully tosses a leaf here or there at him, and one sticks in his hair. Watching them in this simple moment, I feel like I could sit here all day, wrapped up in the splendid happiness of who they are together.

But before I can inhale peacefully at the sight, I clutch my head. A sharp pain radiates from the centre out, a piercing sensation that stabs into every nerve in my head. I squint my eyes shut, the throbbing pain ripping my brain apart, making it hard to think.

My hand massages my scalp, but it's no use. The migraine is back and I can think of nothing else.

When the agony eventually subsides, a dull roar still echoing in my head, I open my eyes to look over at 312 Bristol Lane, hoping there's still a moment to be seen.

But they are gone, presumably back into their cocoon of happiness, their home, and their love.

I rub my head once more, glancing back into my own living room. The house silently screams of coldness, of emptiness, and of something missing.

Chapter 4

I meticulously turn my gold band as I stare at the photograph on top of the stony, dusty fireplace. Amos is asleep on the sofa. I reach out a hand gingerly, almost afraid to touch the glass, afraid if my fingers make contact with it, the fact he's gone will be real.

Time eases the pain and shock of his death, but it doesn't take away the burdens of loneliness and loss. It doesn't make it easier.

For the fourth time today, I touch the chilling glass, eyeing the black and white photograph with both sadness and a smile. In the picture, we're looking at each other, love radiating even without colour. There's a rose bush behind us. I can still see the vibrant reds within the murky grey. One of my delicate hands shoves back the itchy veil from my ravishing curls. He's staring at me as if he wants to devour me, and, if I remember correctly, I think he did want to, judging from the words he was whispering in my ear right after the camera flashed.

It makes me blush just thinking of it.

We were so young, so naive, so in love. I was so happy then.

Time was hard on us, as it is to so many. Still, this picture has always sat on this fireplace, a symbol of that perfect day. Each time I've seen it over the years, it's been like a connection to the past. It's a relic of the love we once had – the carefree, roses-in-the-background kind of love, where starry-eyed lovers think nothing could ever tear them apart.

'So long ago,' I say out loud to the picture, feeling in some ways like that moment was yesterday and in some ways like it was two hundred years ago instead of sixty-seven.

My hands shaking, I squeeze the photograph as if I can clutch on to us, on to the people in the picture. My mind wraps itself around the memories, good and bad, and my chest heaves with the realisation of all that's happened. I'm suddenly desperate to hold on to what I see, and before I can stop myself, I'm squeezing harder and harder. I squeeze until my hand vibrates from the effort. I squeeze until I hear a punchy crack, the glass snapping right in the middle, the line weaving down my body in the photograph, marring the perfect, smiling woman.

I set the cracked memento back down, my hand finding the edge of the mantel now. I stare at my handiwork, the cracks now giving it a new feeling. I don't know why, but it suits the picture. The imperfections make it better. My finger traces the cracked glass for a moment, and I marvel in the pattern, in the new texture, and in the picture that is still very much the same but also a little bit different.

I study the faces I know so well but that somehow seem so distant from me. The glass shifts slightly, leaving part of the picture uncovered. It will fall prey to the elements, to the air of life around it. It's not protected anymore.

Gazing at the photo, I am bombarded with thoughts and ideas, a dull roar making me tired. I listen to the words, trying to home in on the ones to pay attention to, wondering how I got here. Wondering if I could've ever imagined how it would all turn out.

I couldn't have. I would have never known how things would rotate and swirl, spinning into a cacophony of chaos as we drudged through the years. I didn't understand it, even then, how actions have consequences. Or maybe I just didn't want to understand it.

I certainly had experiences. Looking at the eyes of the woman in the photograph, I see what so many didn't.

I see what he didn't.

I see the secrets of a haunted past, of consequences not yet uncovered, of the havoc my actions would reap covered up with a charming smile.

Life flies by. That's the cliché all old people say to the young, but it's so damn true. One minute, you're standing by the rose bushes on your wedding day, wondering what beautiful things life will greet you with. The next, your frail, shaking hand is touching the glass of the past, staring into eyes and skin you don't even recognise anymore, wondering how it all came to pass.

I wipe the single tear that streams down my cheek, and I exhale.

'I miss you,' I say into the crisp October air, wishing like in the movies, a voice could whisper back. But it doesn't. I'm alone, all alone, as usual. There will be no anniversary card from him today. There will be no red roses, no sweet embrace to remind me I'm not alone in this crazy world. Instead, there will be me, Amos and an endless day of nothingness, which has become our tradition.

It doesn't do to dwell on the past. I know that. I know I

have to keep going. Sighing, I lay the photo flat on the mantel, the cracked glass now face down. I tear myself away. I step on the creaking floorboard in the living room as I make my way to my only sanctuary – the rocking chair. I plunk my body down, suddenly regretting the dress slacks and blouse I put on. I don't know what I was thinking this morning when I painstakingly got dressed. It's Wednesday. I have nowhere to be today. It's not grocery shopping day or doctor's appointment day. It's just a stay-at-home Wednesday, even if it is my wedding anniversary. I guess it just seemed respectful to put some effort in. In some crazy part of my mind, I suppose I thought maybe he could see me from wherever he is. It's nuts, I know. But putting on those soft pink slacks and matching blouse made me feel like I was appreciating what today was. It just didn't feel right sitting in my robe.

Nonetheless, as the pants cut into my flesh uncomfortably, I wish I'd stayed in my nightclothes. If you're going to stay home alone, you may as well be comfortable.

That's what conclusion I've come to, anyway, even though my mother liked to tell me in my youth that beauty was pain. Sometimes now I think beauty might be overrated … then again, maybe it's just a result of my unhappiness when I see the pallid skin in the mirror, the fried, grey hair. Maybe it's just wishful thinking that beauty no longer counts, the corpse-like figure who peers back at me far from a thing of beauty.

Out of my peripheral vision, the heavy door to my right, in the centre of the back wall, calls me. Most days, I don't look at it, the barricade efficiently doing its job. The brass doorknob hasn't had fingerprints on it for so long, I don't even know if it would turn.

In some ways, I'd like to think it wouldn't. I'd like to think it's rusted shut, shielding me from what's just beyond the threshold.

A tear comes to my eye as I try to ignore it, try not to look at the door that hasn't been opened in so long, that won't be opened.

Even without looking at it, though, I can see it as if I'm staring at it. I can feel the smooth wood, the stain on it almost tacky. I can feel the imperfections and details, their pattern memorised by my creaky old fingers, which still remember every knot, every rough spot on that door, every detail. I glance down at my fingers as they do a dance on the rocking chair, recalling the shape of the doorknob and its chilling feel on my fingertips.

I take a deep breath, the pain in my chest swelling as I try to push the thought aside.

I've become a master at ignoring it. I walk past that door every day. I see it every day. Yet, a piece of me doesn't see it, doesn't notice it. It's been blacked out.

Why today? Why now? Why does it have to come creeping in, to make me feel even worse?

I shudder, saying out loud, 'Stop it, stop it, stop it. That's enough.' I hold my head, take a deep breath and open my eyes.

There. All's better now.

I rock slowly, my head against the wooden headrest. Amos meows, jumping in the window this time to look out with me. He stares at a robin perched on the picket fence as I study the two-storey across the street. The bird looks so out of place against the rotting leaves. A bird like that belongs in the perfect white snow, a crimson marvel in a sea of plainness.

It flaps and drifts upward and away, landing on the spouting of 312 Bristol Lane.

I smile as I look at the perfect bricks, the adorable little window at the top, the shining windows in the front. It's such a lovely house, made even lovelier by the fact there's a couple there now, a couple I get to study.

I rock in my chair for a while, staring at the house, wondering where they are. The car is gone, and the house is so empty. I realise I'm so lost without them. It's odd being on Bristol Lane all alone yet again. I really don't know how I used to survive when they weren't over there. What did I do with myself? It feels like a lifetime ago.

My mind drifts back, and I think about how not so long ago, the house was always empty, the creaky sign in the front yard begging someone to move in. It felt like ages and ages that 312 Bristol Lane was abandoned, desolate, and lonely. Just like me.

I furrow my brow, massaging my forehead with my thumb and forefinger. Before Bristol Lane, before the empty months, someone lived there. I know they did. I remember there was a couple there for a while, a short while. I remember they left in a hurry on a day not unlike today. Was it last year? Two years ago? Was it October they left or was it summer? Everything's messed up in my head, and I can't seem to set it straight. What happened to them? Why did they leave so quickly? My memory fails me.

But sitting here by myself with nothing to watch, I challenge myself to remember. It's good to push the mind. I shake my head, trying to recall, searching the inner recesses of my brain for faces and names and details. My head starts to ache from the process, but I can't let it go.

Who were they? I can't believe my memory is so hazy. It frustrates me, causing me to rock a little faster, to rub my head a little bit harder.

Think. Remember.

Images come to mind of a couple, a black-haired woman with very tanned skin and an exotic look about her. I see her fuzzily in my mind, the details of her face blurred. She was lean and lanky, but in a model sort of way. She was married, her husband a rather large man. I remember thinking he didn't need any pie. I do know that much.

I recall images of them moving in, angrily yelling in the front lawn. There were no sweet kisses. There was no laughter. They were miserable over there from the beginning. I remember feeling like they didn't deserve a house as grand as 312 Bristol Lane.

I remember sitting here thinking I wished they would just move out, even on day one.

Still, I don't remember the ins and outs of their lives or the details of what they were all about. What did they do all day? What interactions did I witness? I can't really recall. It's hell to get old, for the mind to start to fade. It's crazy what we remember and what we forget.

I rock for a bit more, staring at the house, still trying to jog my memory, but it's not really working. It's like I can't remember a time the sunshine-yellow woman didn't live next door. Maybe it's just that I don't want to remember a time when she didn't. I like them. They bring energy to the street.

The longer I think, though, the more anxious I get. I feel a bit like my skin is crawling, the prickling of the hairs on my arms making me uneasy. I may not remember the last couple so well, but I do get this sense of dread, of heaviness.

And even though I can't remember the details, I do get one overwhelming vibe from my jaunt down memory lane: I don't think I liked them very much.

In fact, the more I stare at the house, the more I'm certain of it. I didn't like them at all, especially her. That dark, luscious hair didn't fool me. She was beautiful on the outside, I know that. But she wasn't a good person.

She was nosy. That's it. I remember. She was so, so nosy. Always looking at me, perusing me like I was some kind of person to keep an eye on. The nerve of her. I've lived here so long, and this young thing moved in and thought she could take over the lane. She thought she could be rude, could get in my business. She was always glaring at me, always staring. And not in a neighbourly way or a curious way. It was in a way that told me she didn't like me.

There were no afternoon teas with that one. There were no sweet gestures or pies or kind exchanges. There were just nosy stares and questions about what I was doing. There was no neighbourly love, I remember now.

I was so glad when they left. Surprised but glad. Did they leave in the middle of the night? I think they did. If my memory serves me correctly, which in fairness it doesn't always, I think one morning I got up and the couple from 312 Bristol Lane were gone. They must've packed their belongings in the night and left like some scoundrels disappearing under the cover of darkness.

I knew she shouldn't be trusted from day one. And I was right.

I guess none of it really matters now, though, in truth. Because those neighbours weren't even important. The new people in 312 Bristol Lane are all that matters. I'm glad the other couple left so early. These two suit me so much better.

Still, I wonder what happened to them, the old neighbours. Where are they now? Is life working out as they planned?

I've lived long enough to know that life has a way of working out differently, no matter who you are. And now, the couple across the street get a chance to live out their story here, me bearing witness. I hope they get it right. I hope they make the story a good one. I hope they don't turn out to be scoundrels. I hope with all my heart they find the life they want.

But even as the thought dances in my deepest wishes, I look down to see my hands slightly shaking. They deserve happiness ... but will they get it? Will they find a way to make it work?

I inhale deeply, clutching my hands together in a prayer-like pose, trying to calm down the tremors.

It can happen. They can make it work. They can find the life I couldn't. They can make their own happiness, can't they? It's possible. It's certainly possible. But then again, life doesn't always work out how you hoped.

* * *

It's dinnertime. I spent the morning in my chair, of course, with my cup of tea. At noon, I watched my soap operas and read the newspaper. I even grabbed my favourite novel, *Gone With the Wind*. I was feeling literary today I guess, the dusty pages dog-eared from being reread so many times. After all, I was so bored today with the couple from 312 Bristol Lane gone. I wish I knew where they went, if for no other reason than to entertain my mind today with fancy visions of them doing whatever it is they're doing. I hope they did something fun.

I was sitting in my rocking chair, flipping through the pages of my book with Amos on my lap when they came home. The car pulled into the driveway. It was late afternoon when they returned, smiling and holding hands up the walkway before heading inside. They looked good, happier than usual. I smiled at the sight of their return, the sun lowering on the horizon. I was so glad they were back. I closed my book and studied them, waiting to see what the view would uncover today.

It makes me a little sad that my day depends so much on their actions. How crazy that my mood clearly improved when they came home. Then again, they are the only sense of life left in my days. They're the only things that remind me of what it means to do more than simply exist. Maybe I just need to escape from this house, from the memories – and from the date.

I have a cup of tea in my hands now as I settle back into the rocking chair. I ate a quick meal at the table, mainly to stretch my legs a bit. I found myself hurrying, though, to get my eating over with. I wanted to get back here so I didn't miss anything. I hardly got to see any of them today, so I want to make the most of tonight.

Darkness looms as I settle in, studying the changing sky. A few birds are flying about, left and right, the impending night inciting them to head for home. Amos lets out a meow before plodding off to his cat bed in the corner of the room.

I stay put.

They're having dinner tonight in the dining room.

It seems they only have dinner there once in a while. They have a tiny table in their kitchen, too.

She's gone above and beyond today, though. There are beautiful candles adding a soft glow to the room. With the encroaching darkness, it's getting even easier to see the scene. She still hasn't put blinds or curtains up. I hope she keeps it that way. The glass is a little bit dingier now, time passing and caking a thin veil of dirt and dust on the pane. Still, my view is almost unobstructed. Maybe she'll wash the windows soon and my view will be improved.

She's wearing royal blue tonight, a satiny finish on the top of her dress gleaming beautifully in the eerie glow of the candlelight. The light dances off her face, her hair swept upward in an elegant style. Her dark lipstick painted on her perfectly shaped lips contrasts with her pale skin in a way that is arrestingly gorgeous. I can't stop watching her as she carefully places items on the table, a graceful domestic dance.

Next, she puts a casserole in the centre of the table, fidgeting with her hair after she does. It seems like she has a bunch of different dishes on the table. I wonder what she's made and if she's a good cook. She disappears for a moment, walking back with a basket between her two hands, golden bread rolls stacked up towards her chin. I wonder if she made them from scratch. They're the best, after all. They're so worth the work, even if they are tedious. My mouth waters at the thought of the homemade rolls I always made, the ones that practically melted in my mouth.

Eventually, he comes in, and she gives him a peck on the cheek. He loosens the black tie around his neck, the white collar on his shirt standing at attention. They sit across from each other, the long table in between them, each at the head seats so they are sideways to me. They each hold up a glass of champagne or wine or some other drink and toast. The candlelight dances between them, the glow of the room warm yet oppressive at the same time.

I wonder what their toast is. I hope it's something sweet. She should say something like, 'To an amazing night with a man who makes every day a special occasion.'

Okay, so that's a little cheesy, I know. But I think she should say something to make him know he's special, that every single day with him is special.

It's not my toast to give though, so I just sit, studying them, not knowing what she decides on. I'm sure it's lovely. I'm sure it will do.

There is a shuffling of dishes as they heap their plates, passing around the casserole and laughing. She has a wide smile, and her head flies back at several moments in laughter. He's a good storyteller; I can tell. He talks with his hands, just like her. Good storytellers, I think, should talk with their hands.

Plus, he makes eye contact with her when he's telling a story. I always liked that. You need to look into someone's eyes to really speak to them. It's a skill so many ignore.

I watch the scene, a peaceful scene, as the moon rises over their house. They take their time, languishing over dinner. I'm glad to see they're appreciating the meal, that they're taking a moment to just slow down. They're always rushing about, to and fro. I like that they're focusing on each other, even if just for tonight.

After a while, he gets up from the table, putting his napkin down. He crosses the distance between them casually, in a couple of strides. Standing before her, he offers her his hand,

and I smile at the gesture. I love an impromptu dance. More than that, I love a man who isn't afraid to dance without a reason, to dance around the dining room table on a Wednesday evening.

She shakes her head as if she's embarrassed, looking down at the plate in front of her.

I will her to change her mind. *Don't say no. Please don't say no. You'll regret it someday if you do. Someday, you'll wish you had danced with him every chance you got. Someday, you'll give anything to feel his hands on your waist, to have him twirling you around that table in a fit of laughter.*

And for a moment, I think I'm losing my mind because, as if she's heard my whispered prayer, she looks up from the table, turns her head and stares directly at me. I feel our eyes lock, my stomach flipping at the odd sensation pulsing through me as she stares. It's like her eyes pierce through me, body and soul. I'm so uncomfortable, yet I can't look away. After a long moment of her staring, no smile, her face steadfast, she glances back to the scene playing out.

With some coaxing, she eventually nods and takes his hand. She doesn't say 'no' today. I exhale the breath I didn't realise I was holding, shaking my head.

Did I imagine it? Certainly, she hadn't been looking at me, had she?

I brush off the chill in my veins, focusing instead on the beautiful scene unfolding before me now. They lean in to each other, dancing by the candlelit table like two lovers who just uncovered the truth between them, his hand finding the waist of her satiny blue dress, her head resting on his shoulder.

I close my eyes, partially because I feel like this intimate moment should be between the two of them only, and partially because I'm drifting back to one of the many dances by the dining room table I had.

Our song plays in my head, that jazzy, big band song. He sings it to me in my ear, his hot breath sending chills down my spine.

* * *

'This is crazy,' I said, giggling wildly.

'This is perfect,' he said.

'I have dishes to do,' I argued.

'They can wait.' He kissed my cheek, then my forehead and finally my lips. We kissed for a long time, the magic of the first wedded year dancing in our hearts.

The dishes didn't get done that night, but it was okay. Instead of chores or responsibilities, we spent the night revelling in the beauty of our love, in our connection and in each other.

Then, our early dance morphs into another scene, a scene from later in our marriage.

'Dance with me,' he said, holding out his hand. He started humming the familiar song.

'I can't,' I replied, icily, averting my gaze to the ground. Tears formed, burning the inner corners of my mascara-laden eyes.

'Please, honey. Don't do this. I love you. I know things are tough right now.'

'Tough? You have no idea what tough is. There you are, pretending things are great, but in the meantime, I'm devastated. How can you even suggest we dance, like nothing's happened? Like nothing's changed?'

'But, baby, it hasn't. It doesn't have to. Just dance with me. I love you. I've always loved you and only you.'

I looked up to see his pleading eyes this time. They sobered me, but the anger wouldn't let go. I knew it was misplaced. I knew none of it was really his fault, and maybe a piece of me knew I was being slightly insane. He loved me; I knew this.

But it wasn't enough. He just wasn't enough then.

The hurt and denial intensified. It whirred within me. I tossed my linen napkin on the table, kicked the leg of the wooden heirloom and stormed to the kitchen.

'I need to finish the dishes,' I bellowed. And with that, the dance never happened, the song left unsung as the stark silence filled the growing void between us.

* * *

I open my eyes, tears flowing again. They're still dancing, the moment not lost.

'Dance with him always. Every time. Don't let anything stop you,' I whisper into the darkness, a silent prayer for the couple. If only there had been someone to warn me. If only I had danced when he asked.

But the 'if onlys' can't change anything. All they do is make an old lady lose her mind a little more, make her lose sight of the good. I've got to let it go.

So, standing, I call for Amos as I trudge up the stairs to slip into my nightclothes and put another evening behind me. Another wedding anniversary is over, and I've survived. Sometimes, after all, survival is the best we can hope to achieve.

Chapter 5

I'm taking a break from the window today. It doesn't do an old woman any good to completely absorb herself in another life. My own days may not be exciting anymore, the sparkle of youth long gone, but I need to live them as best I can. I need to get up, move around, do things. I have no choice.

Well, I suppose there is always a choice. But right now, I think the only choice I can reasonably make is to keep pushing through, like I've done for so many years.

I decide, with a sigh, to do some cleaning today. The house isn't very dirty, it's true. When you live alone, there aren't any people to pick up after, many dishes to wash, many beds to make, or much dirt to clean. There are no lawn clippings tracked in on his shoes to swipe up or coffee cups scattered about to tend to. Life alone is decidedly less messy, although I'm no longer certain that's something to be happy about. In my younger days, I hated cleaning. I would yell at him for leaving his socks around, for leaving dirty plates on the end table. I was frustrated to no end that no matter what I did, the house was never clean.

Now, the house is too clean. Other than the dusky smell from age and time passing, other than the stale air from the doors and windows being shut, it's pretty much the same as it's been for years. Not a picture is moved, not a new decorative display has been added. What's the point? In many ways, this draughty house is a mausoleum for the past, so little having been changed in so many decades.

Still, I feel like I need to do something that seems productive even if it really isn't. I have nervous energy building, and I need to burn it somehow. I want to get rid of it before it builds up anymore.

I stumble towards the cleaning closet and stoop to get the duster. My back aches as I lean down, but I try to ignore it.

Amos meows at my feet as I head towards the living room, ready to crack every piece of dust there is, ready to swipe it all away.

Twenty minutes later, sweat beads on my forehead. I've managed to dust all the pictures and shelves on the left half of the room. I'm huffing a little, out of breath from the stretching and bending. It's pathetic.

I take a seat, duster in hand, frustrated with myself. I can't even do things I hate, like cleaning. There's so little left I can do, even when I'm feeling up to it.

I sit, staring at the broken photograph that still lies flat on the mantel. I don't need to look at it to know the curve of my lips, the lines of his stance. It's seared into my memory like a scorching flame.

I think about all the times we fought in this room – about dusting, about him pulling his weight, about all sorts of decisions. I think about his eye rolls that would infuriate me, all the times he tried to tell me to calm down. Sometimes, I savoured the chance to get to him, to push his buttons. Such is marriage, I suppose – annoying each other, getting angry. It's not all perfect, you know.

In the middle of my dusting depression, there's a knock at the door. For a moment, I think maybe I'm hearing things; it wouldn't be the first time. Maybe Amos jumped on the counter or maybe something fell. But no, there's another gentle rap, rap, rap, and it's clearly coming from the front door.

Energised by the possibility of a visitor, which rarely happens, I pick myself up from the couch, tossing the duster to the floor. I'll retrieve it later.

'Coming,' I yell in a voice hoarse from age and time. I mindlessly fluff my hair and try to smooth my shirt. I will my feet to shuffle faster.

In my youth, I used to be afraid to open the door, afraid a serial killer or a burglar would try to weasel his way in. I always made my husband go. In the past couple years, though, I've realised two things.

First, there's no one else to answer the door now.

And second, at my age, who cares if it is a burglar or a serial killer? Maybe it would make things interesting. That's the one good thing about getting old – fear wanes a bit because really, what is there to fear? Death? It's knocking on my door anyway.

Not literally, though. Because when I open the door, I smile. It's her: Jane from 312 Bristol Lane.

'Hi there, can I come in?' she asks. She's got a delicate scarf wrapped around her neck to keep out the biting chill of the autumn air.

'Of course. I was just doing some pesky housework.' I extend my hand towards the interior of the house, ushering her in from the brisk air. I'm surprised she's here, but also excited to have some company. You don't always realise how lonely you've been until the chance to talk to another person arises. I've never been one to complain when someone interrupted my cleaning. The rest of the dusting can wait for another day.

She steps over the threshold, getting ready to kick off her shoes on the rug inside the doorway that masks the hardwood, protecting it from what, I don't know. 'You don't have to take them off, really. It's fine. Come in. Can I get you some tea?'

'Tea would be lovely. If you show me where it is, I can make it.'

I want to say no and be a good host. I want to tell her it isn't a bother, that I can make her tea. But my hands are aching from all the damn dusting, and I'm out of breath. So I smile and nod, leading her slowly to the kitchen.

Amos meows, rubbing Jane's legs as she makes a fuss over him.

'You like cats?' I ask.

'Love them. I've always wanted one, but my husband's allergic.'

I give a sympathetic nod as I point her towards the tea cupboard. 'Everything is in there, dear, and the kettle is on the stove.'

I pull out a chair and have a seat, feeling like a lump on a log sitting here while company makes tea in my own house. Watching her move gracefully, though, her long, slender body stretching to reach the tea and then to fill the kettle with water in the sink, I smile. It feels good to have someone here to care for me, even if it is just a cup of tea. I can't remember the last time someone ventured in and spent some time with me. It's been years and years. Who would come to visit, after all? That's a terribly sad thought, I realise, and decide not to think about it. Instead, I choose to focus on the beauty of the fact

I finally do have someone to visit with me and to make me tea. It's really a lovely thing.

I study her, realising that the stoic stare the other day must have been in my imagination. How foolish I was to think she was anything but kind and sweet. She's lovely, inside and out. Looking at her in my kitchen, I can't imagine anything but warmth radiating from her.

I shake my head, telling myself I need to get it together. It wouldn't do to lose my mind at this stage of the game.

She picks out two teabags.

'Put them in after. You put the teabag in after,' I say when she tries to put it in the cup first.

She turns to look at me, wordlessly setting down the teabag.

I breathe a sigh of relief. No use messing with routine now.

'It's lovely of you to stop by,' I say once she's got the kettle on and has a seat across from me.

She smiles. 'Sorry it's been so long. You know how it is. Busy and all that,' she says, waving her hand.

I nod and smile, not wanting to ruin the moment by telling her I have no clue what she's talking about. Because I don't these days. Busy for me is having to retrieve the mail from the slot or make a single phone call. Busy isn't really in my vocabulary anymore, the sleepy pace of life I've become accustomed to seeming quite sad.

But busy *was* in my vocabulary at one time, so I choose to speak from that point of reference. 'Life's so hectic, huh?'

'It is.'

'Everyone's right, you know. It flies by. Really does.'

'That's what they all tell me. Some days, though, with the washing and cooking and all that, it's kind of hard to believe.'

Her smile, carefully outlined in a gorgeous hue of lipstick, is wide, softening the words.

'I always hated chores. It's the one bonus of being a lonely old woman – you don't have to worry about keeping up appearances, you know?'

She reaches across to pat my hand. I shouldn't have laid on the lonely part. I don't want pity. But she smiles. 'Yeah, well, not many people to keep up appearances for these days. We barely know anyone in this town.'

I see a hint of sadness in her eyes and wonder what it's all about.

Then again, I seem to recognise it. The haze of the honeymoon stage is dulling a bit and the knowledge of wifely duties is setting in for her. It isn't easy sacrificing your identity to be part of a duo. I get it. I had so many days when I, too, wondered why. What was the point of it all? Was laundry, cooking dinner and sex once in a while really what life had come to? It's a struggle painted on her face, one I understand even after all these years.

'Don't you have friends in the area?' I prod, curious now, wanting to give her a chance to vent.

She shrugs. 'Not really. I'm originally from out of the area. I met my husband, we fell in love and, before I knew it, I was packing up my bags and leaving everyone I knew. I didn't mind. He's a good enough man. Handsome, good job. It's just – a little lonely sometimes, you know?'

'I know, dear. But you'll make friends. Are you working?'

'No. I'm a full-time housewife. Seemed like it made the most sense for us, you know? I'm hoping to have kids soon, start a family.'

'That's lovely,' I say, a smile taking over.

'How about you, do you have any kids?' she asks as she stands to tend to the boiling kettle and make our tea.

I sigh, fidgeting with my ring. Pressure builds in my chest, a pain throbbing. I inhale and exhale, telling myself it's okay. It isn't her fault. It's an innocent question. 'No, no kids. It was just my husband and me. I'm the only one left now, obviously.'

She turns, pausing from the tea pouring. 'I'm so sorry, I didn't know.'

My wedding ring turns slowly in between the fingers of my right hand, spinning round and round as my foot taps. I look up at Jane, though, and am grounded in the fact she didn't know. How could she?

I force the fake smile I've used so many times to the forefront and reassure her. 'It's fine. Besides, it's not like it's a secret. I'm doing okay, really. I've learned to make peace with it.'

She looks at me, a long look, and I can tell she wants to ask something but is debating. I want to nudge her forward, but I don't want to be pushy. I get the sense she's ... I don't know what. But I get this creeping suspicion I need to be careful with her, watch my tongue. I don't want to push her away. It would be terrible to push her away.

She turns the conversation now to autumn and Mark's Mart and the price of strawberries as she brings the tea over. We laugh and talk like two old friends for the next couple of hours, sipping our tea in between laughter and the exchange of stories.

When she leaves and the house is empty, I realise how much she filled it when she was here. I realise how much I'd missed having friends, having conversation, having connection. Just having someone to sip some weak tea with on a dull afternoon. Someone to give me an excuse to stop dusting for. The time went so quickly with her there. I forget sometimes how having someone to talk to really does make the day go faster. I miss that.

I also realise she never quite said why she stopped by. It was sort of odd timing, her showing up out of the blue.

I don't care, though. Because she can come back anytime. Maybe she's just lonely too. Maybe she feels the need to do a good deed or do some penance by visiting a clearly isolated old lady. Whatever her reasoning, I hope she comes back, because as I lower myself into the tub very carefully later that night, I note that I feel peaceful for the first time in years.

And when I crawl under the covers, settling my head onto the lumpy, familiar pillow later, I don't think about the black emptiness of the room or the cold, empty spot beside me. I simply think about Jane's smile, her laugh and how much I hope she returns.

It's good to have a friend, after all. I've always needed a friend, especially now.

Life is hard. Life isn't perfect. We all have our regrets, something I know all too well. Sometimes it takes another person to help us overcome those regrets, those feelings, that darkness. And even now, in this stage of my life, I'm surrounded by plenty of dark regrets.

I could use a friend indeed. Maybe Jane is exactly the person to be just that.

Chapter 6

I was seven the first time I realised the world is a lonely place. In truth, I should've learned it years before that. My perfect place in the world was tainted the day Lucy came into my life. I just didn't know it at the time. Of course, I'd been too young when she was born to know the difference between right and wrong, just and unjust, loved and not loved.

When I was seven, though, things became apparently clear: I was no longer important in the family. Or maybe, in truth, I never was.

We stood on the altar looking out at all the people. My eyes landed on my parents, sitting five pews back. I counted the five rows with pride, double-checking to make sure I'd counted correctly. I'd been working on my numbers, on my counting. My teacher said I was a smart girl. I'd beamed with pride that she'd noticed.

Lucy stood beside me, her red satin dress shining under the streams of sunlight as the preacher spoke about something I wasn't listening to. I was too busy watching Mom and Dad. Dad was in his best shirt and slacks, his jacket frayed at the edges but still looking great. Mom was in my favourite dress, the blue one with pink flowers. She looked beautiful, even with her hair swept back.

We'd been picked along with some other children in the church to perform a song. It was a special moment because I was getting to sing the solo. It was my mom's favourite song, too: 'The Old Rugged Cross'. I'd memorised the words. I'd practised over and over. I couldn't wait for my moment to shine.

This was going to be my moment. I imagined Mom and Dad beaming with pride, rushing up after the song to hug me, Dad lifting me into the air like he had when I was younger, before Lucy became their sole focus. They'd crowd around me, praising me for a job well done. After church, we'd all gather in the hall and they'd be grinning ear to ear, telling everyone I was their daughter.

The preacher grew quiet, and I knew it was time. I fidgeted with the skirt on my blue-checked dress. Mom told me the mustard stain on the hem wasn't noticeable. Still, I tucked the fabric over itself, clutching it with a hand to cover it. I needed everything to be perfect.

The song began, our Sunday school teacher leading us as we sang the words in our makeshift choir. Lucy sang too loudly, as usual, her voice shrieking out the words. At one point, she stepped in front of me, shoving me over. I shoved her back slightly, knowing my moment to sing was coming up. I needed to be the centre of attention for once. I needed to be in the middle, noticed, for when it was my turn.

She stepped forward again, right in front of me, and anger bubbled. It was just like her to try to steal the spotlight all the time. In school, at home, when we were baking with Mom – she was always stealing my spotlight. She was always making sure I was shoved to the side.

Not today, I thought to myself. It was my solo. I needed this moment, had waited for it all week.

I elbowed her in the ribs, inching forward as the song came to my solo. It was a soft shove, not enough to do any damage but enough to show her where she belonged.

I opened my mouth to belt out the words, but at that moment, Lucy screamed, falling to the ground, tumbling down the steps of the altar.

'Ow, you hurt me,' she whined, flailing on the ground and pointing up at me.

The organ continued playing, but the words for my solo eluded me. I didn't sing. I watched in horror as the teacher rushed over, helping Lucy from the ground and asking if she was okay. My parents, too, rushed from their pews.

Couldn't they see she wasn't really hurt? That I hadn't done anything? That she'd started it?

The other kids laughed and pointed at the ruckus, ignoring the song. 'The Old Rugged Cross' went unsung, the preacher looking angry. The whole church stared at me. I was in the centre of the altar, feeling so alone, my face burning with embarrassment and frustration.

And eventually, that embarrassment and frustration boiled over into something else entirely: rage.

My parents helped Lucy up, her crocodile tears rolling down her cheeks. Mom hurried over, grabbing me by the wrist and yanking me down from the altar in front of everyone.

'You've done it now,' she hissed through clenched teeth.

And instead of them congratulating me, they dragged me from the church as everyone watched, kids on the altar laughing and pointing as the preacher tried to regain composure and order.

Outside the church, the sun was shining, the clouds billowy and soft. Mom's hold on my wrist hurt, but I didn't dare cry out.

I was too stunned, too shattered to complain anyway. My stomach burned and my head pounded. How did this happen? How could this happen?

It was her. It was always her. I seethed inside as she held Dad's hand. He comforted her, telling her it was all okay.

They rushed us to the car and Dad tucked Lucy safely in the back. I was shaking now, out of frustration and fear of what would come. Dad didn't like to be humiliated.

Before I could open the door, he took one arm and slammed me up against the back of the car. Mom crawled inside, ignoring the scene unfolding.

'You bitch. How dare you embarrass us. Look what you've done. You're ruining this family. You ruin everything,' he said, his face inches from mine.

Tears welled, stinging my eyes.

'Daddy, it wasn't me. She did it. She started it. She shoved me.' My voice was shaky as I pleaded with him. I needed him to understand, just this once. I wanted him to side with me and to understand that it was all Lucy. It was always Lucy.

There was no sense of understanding that day, however. There was no pride or acknowledgement of what today was supposed to be about. Instead, he shoved against me, his arm pressing against my chest, making it hard to breathe. I felt the metal of the car, hot from the sun, against my back.

'You're the older one. You should know better. Don't you dare blame Lucy. She's an angel. You're nothing. You're the problem. We'd have been better off without you. Now get in the car.' He pressed against me one last time, his rage jolting through the pressure he placed on me.

As he stepped back, I slumped to the ground, but he grabbed me by the hair, yanking me up and tossing me in the car. I crumpled on the seat, in shock even though I really shouldn't have expected anything different. It wasn't the first time I'd felt Mom or Dad's unhinged wrath.

The whole way home, I shook with terror, with anger, with a sense that all was not right. I stared out the window, watching the familiar landscapes whir by as the car sped onward, back to the home that had always housed so many dark truths for me, even at seven.

What had happened to me? Why had everything changed? Why was I never good enough?

The questions swirled over and over in my head, looping through clips of memories and of other times I'd felt this bubbling anger inside. I thought about how Lucy was always the one to get new clothes while mine fell apart into tattered rags. I thought about the beaming smiles when she came home with a good report from her teacher and the ignorance or wave of a hand when I did the same. I thought about all the signs I'd tried too hard to ignore but couldn't any longer.

I was nothing. She was everything.

Although I was the eldest, there was never a doubt: she was first; I was second.

Sitting beside Lucy, a scalding fury stirred in me. I thought about how I could get payback. I considered lopping the head off her favourite doll or drowning it in the river next time we were outside. I imagined putting bugs in her shoes or cutting her hair when she was sleeping. I thought about what it would feel like to pin her against the car like Dad had done to me, to keep pressing, overpowering her, showing her just how strong I was. It became clear to me as we turned onto the familiar street that I wanted, no needed, revenge.

She needed to pay.

When we got home and everyone got out of the car, Dad still seething mad, I trudged to my room, tears falling from my eyes.

Lucy strutted into my room, her satiny dress still perfectly crisp.

'Sorry about your solo,' she murmured, mocking me and mimicking me with the whiny voice that made me want to choke her.

I stared at her, my chest heaving with rage. I crossed the floor of the room and she backed up, perhaps seeing something in me she hadn't noticed before.

'Sorry,' she murmured, shaking a little now, but I didn't stop.

I kept creeping towards her as she inched backwards into the corner.

'I'll scream for my mom,' she said, and the way she said 'my', like she was claiming her as her own, did something to me. It made something snap.

Maybe because I'd known it was the truth.

I put my arm against her tiny chest, shoving her hard against the wall in the bedroom, pushing and pushing, thinking about how hard I could push. Her breathing was ragged and she was crying now. I stared into her face, watching the fear in her eyes and feeling relief that she hadn't won, that I could still win.

Finally, after a long moment, my arms grew weak, shaking from the exertion and the sheer adrenaline. It was only when the strength left my body that I realised I needed to stop. I let up, releasing her. She ran out of the room, panting, and I slumped to the floor, feeling horrible in so many ways as the emotions surrounding my violent victory faded.

What had happened? What had I done?

I sobbed myself to sleep that night. I cried for the lost solo, for my lost parents and for my lost temper.

Most of all, I cried because I realised the anger burning inside wasn't okay.

And because I wasn't sure if I would be able stop it again.

Chapter 7

She comes over several times a week now.

At first, I felt terrible about it, maybe even a little uneasy. I should've never gone on and on about not having kids. She probably just feels obligated or pities me. I don't want anyone feeling sorry for me. I've always found it to be a detestable emotion, reserved for the weakest of the weak.

I have to admit, though, she never makes me feel like it's an imposition. Her smile is always gentle, soothing, when she comes through the door. We have tea together and chat. A few times, she's even stayed to watch the soap operas with me. I feel a connection to her, despite our age difference.

I know she's got her own life, and I know I should tell her she doesn't have to keep coming over. But I can't. Because, suddenly, I'm not so isolated. Suddenly, getting out of bed in the morning isn't so difficult. Suddenly, I feel like a little piece of me is back.

So what do an old lady and a young, perky blonde talk about, you ask?

Everything. We talk about everything.

The weather and the grocery store – that's where it started. But as we spend time together, getting to know each other, we've come to realise we have so much to talk about.

We talk about how we both want to visit Paris someday. We talk about the actors on our soap operas and predict what's coming next. We talk about Amos and how she wants a cat too. We talk about muffin recipes and cleaning tips and books we've both read.

It's quite lovely having a friend after all this time. It's exhilarating to have companionship, to have someone to share things with. I didn't realise how much I've missed it.

Today, we're making a pie.

Mostly, she's making a pie – rhubarb, of course, because what other kind of pie is even worth it? I'm standing nearby, my shaky hands and aching legs of little use other than handing her ingredients. I have to pass the flour bag with two hands – two hands. It's disgraceful.

I don't have time for self-pity, though, because Jane animatedly chats and chats and chats.

'So, darling, what are you thinking of the neighbourhood now that you've been here a bit?' I ask as she works on the crust.

She smiles. 'It's a nice area. At first, I was taken back by the seclusion of it, you know? With us being the only people on the lane, it felt a little eerie. But now that we know each other, it doesn't feel so lonely, huh?'

I smile and nod. 'Agreed. It was quite uncanny before you moved in. It just felt unnatural, you know? This lovely lane with no children playing on the sidewalk, no cute little families out and about. I'd adapted, of course, gotten used to it over the months the house sat empty. But I was so glad when you moved in. You brought life back to Bristol Lane,' I admit, readjusting my glasses as I stare at her.

She nods. 'Thanks. We try, I guess. I like how quiet it is,

56

but I agree it can be a little too quiet sometimes. A little dull during the day, if I'm being honest. Sometimes, I don't know, I wonder if this is really it, you know?'

I sigh. I know. I know all too well she's not talking about our empty street or the lack of noise. I know she's talking about everything – her, them, life in general.

'It's okay. I know all about it. Being a housewife isn't a walk in the park, and sometimes men are just daft when it comes to understanding our feelings. Sometimes people in general are quite daft. It's a tough world.'

'I know. I guess I'm just edgy, too. I just ... We've been married a while now. I thought by now, things would be different. It's not really going according to plan.' She pauses from rolling out the pie dough and fiddles with the ring on her hand as I watch. There's dough stuck on her wedding band.

'How do you mean?' I ask as I walk over to the kitchen chair, my breathing intensifying despite the short distance to the chair. It's one of those days when everything tires me.

She continues rolling out the dough.

'I guess family is what I mean. I thought by now maybe we'd have a family.'

'Oh? You really want kids, huh?' It's a wasted question because just looking at her as she talks, I know the answer. Of course she wants kids. She wants them as badly as she wants to breathe. It's all over her face.

She pauses, hands on the rolling pin. For a moment, my blood goes cold because I have a flashback to the icy gaze I've seen – no, the icy gaze I thought I'd seen – her emit. I see her face go dark, her eyes narrow in on me. I see a rage frothing beneath that wickedly convincing smile.

Fear simmers to the surface, just beneath my sense of composure.

Just as I'm ready to convince myself I'm not crazy, that she's definitely got a sharp edge to her, the calm, soothing Jane returns. What's wrong with me? Am I going mad?

I rock in my chair a little, readjusting. I don't take my eyes off her.

She turns to me, her smile a little too wide. 'I do. It just feels right, you know? I mean, I didn't have the best family growing up. Mom was a control freak, to put it mildly, and, well, things were ... let's just say really complicated. Not the best, in truth. I just always dreamed of having my own, doing it right – or as right as one can. I wanted a chance to sort of ... redeem my childhood through my own child. I know that makes no sense. I just want to prove I can do it right. But it's been over a year now and doctors are saying it might not happen.'

She's got a faraway look now, her hands still frozen on the rolling pin.

Is it just me or are her hands shaking slightly, the tremors palpable from here despite her attempt to steady them?

She reaches up and smooths a blonde strand, swiping it away from her eye, some white, powdery flour clinging to the strands like snow.

I sigh. I want to convince her it's going to be okay. I should convince her it's going to be okay. But I don't know. I'm not one to help in this department.

'I'm sure it'll work out like it should, you know?' I offer weakly, not really sure what else to say. My gaze falls to my feet, focusing on the small imperfection in the flooring that's been there for decades. I study the crevice, my eyes dancing along the line as I take deep breaths.

'Yeah,' she replies absent-mindedly.

'Well, I'm going to take that back,' I say, refocusing on her. I need to be honest. 'I hope it works out. But if it doesn't, know it's okay not to be okay with it. I had a hard time with it all, to tell you the truth. I think even though I have come to terms with it, some days are still harder than others. I still struggle with aspects of it, I guess.'

Her hands leave the rolling pin then. She wraps herself up in them, as if she's cradling herself, flour now on her shirt. The specks of flour and dough dotting her top bother me. I feel a need to cross the kitchen and bat at the spots, but I don't.

She eyes me, leaning on the counter. 'You couldn't conceive?'

Now it's my turn to wrap myself in my arms in defence. How do I broach this subject? And why, after all this time, is it still so hard?

I slump backwards in the chair, taking a ragged breath and exhaling audibly before continuing. 'It's complicated. But we never had children, and for a long time, I tried to fool myself into thinking it wasn't an issue. But it was. And it built into bigger issues. It took me a long time to realise not having kids ... well, it set my life on a different path, and not a good one like all those motivational speakers would like you to believe. It's hard. So I understand the stress you're under.' I pick at a sharp edge on my fingernail and bite my lip. After all this time, the words are still unbearable to utter. The admission of how badly I wanted it and how much it hurt when it didn't come true – it's a bitter pill, one I haven't ever been able to swallow, even now as an old lady. And I've swallowed a lot of pills over the years. This one – it's different.

She nods slightly, turns and finishes up the crust and the

filling in silence, no words passing between us. I guess we're both lost in thoughts – in sadness, in dreams and in the past.

Finally, after she's whipped the pie together, she pops it into the oven, wiping her hands on her apron. She turns to me, solemn. 'Thank you. It's refreshing to have someone understand. Everyone else is just trying to be all positive.'

'Your husband, too?' I ask as she moves the pie tools to the sink and starts the kettle for tea.

She exhales, rolling her eyes. 'Especially my husband. Telling me to just believe, to pray. Like that's going to magically make this problem disappear. Sometimes he's just so naive, you know? When I first met him, I thought he was this charming, charismatic and intellectual man. Now, I don't know.' Her voice oozes with contempt, with edginess.

I get it, I do. It's a stressful time in life when you want something so badly but can't get it. It's hard to avoid taking it out on those around you. I think you search for reasons, for someone to be culpable because otherwise, it drives you a little crazy.

'I hope you don't blame him for this,' I blurt out, wishing I could take it back. Why did I say that?

'Really? You too?' She glares at me, shaking her head. Her voice is punctuated with iciness. 'He's been on my last nerve about how he thinks I blame him. I don't. I'm not a bad person. We all have our struggles. I hate how he's making this about him. What about me? How about what I'm feeling? Why does he get to play the victim?' She lines up our cups on the table, handles pointing perfectly to the right at ninety degrees, but it's a struggle. Her hands are visibly shaking now, the reckless pulsating of her fingers wildly contrasting with the steadiness of her stance. After persistence and sheer determination, she manages to get the cups in the exact positions she wants them in. It's like this is the most important task she's ever completed; perhaps focusing her mind on this is helping her to escape from the imprisoning anger she feels.

Silence ensues again, this time riddled with tension and words unspoken. I trace a mark on the table with my finger, willing the right words to come to mind. They don't. I don't know what to say. In truth, I don't think there is anything I can say to make it better, which is a hard realisation to accept.

The kettle screams and she perfunctorily removes it, pouring the water into the cups and placing a single teabag in each one. She's quiet as she works, which is unlike her.

I feel horrible that I can't do anything to ease this. I also feel bad for her husband. Such a tenuous subject to have to tiptoe around while dealing with his own feelings over it. The whole situation is a madness few can understand.

He must understand, though, how stressful this is on some level. Certainly, this sweet woman is just having a bad moment. It will pass. They'll find a way through. She'll find a way.

'So, did you watch the soap operas yesterday?' she asks, changing the subject. There is a new chipper tone to her voice, as if we've completely switched gears. Maybe that's just what she needs.

I play along. 'I did.'

'What did you think of Jessica's choice?'

I mentally try to flash back to yesterday. Did I fall asleep during them? Sometimes, they're so repetitive and boring, I just zone out. Usually, I can zone back in twenty minutes later – or twenty days later – and it's the same thing. But Jessica isn't ringing a bell.

'Terrible, terrible story,' I say, not having any clue but not wanting to admit my incompetence. I don't want her thinking I have memory issues. Then again, maybe I don't want to believe I have memory issues.

'I thought the same thing,' she replies, raising a cup of tea to her lips, blowing on it to cool it as I warm my hands on the cup she passed to me.

And as she looks at me, smiling, I shudder a little even though I don't understand why. There's something unsettling in the way she can switch gears so easily, how her sadness can meld into a sweet smile so quickly. There's something unnerving in her eyes, a darkness flashing for the briefest of moments.

I try to shove it aside. When you have so much time to think, sometimes your mind goes to dark places unnecessarily. Sometimes you overanalyse, see things that aren't there. I don't trust my mind one hundred per cent these days. An ageing mind is sometimes a faulty one. *I'm just being crazy*, I tell myself. Certainly, that's it.

Despite my best efforts to quell my uneasiness, though, I can't. She sips her still-scalding tea and I stare, the queasiness in my stomach undeniable. For the first time, I inexplicably feel like Jane isn't as sunshine yellow as I once thought. Suddenly, something seems off, seems weird – and it isn't just her unhappiness over her lack of a family. There's more to it, there's something different.

Is it in her lips, the way they sometimes stretch too widely over her perfectly white teeth in a smile that feels both unnatural and suspicious?

Is it in the whiplash of her emotions, from rage to sadness to happy in minutes?

Or is the way her hands shake, outwardly showing the bubbling of emotion within?

No. These things make me wary, for sure. But it's something else, I realise.

She has wild eyes, ones I've seen before. Ones I thought I'd never see again. They seem to convey a truth her lips, words and actions try to cover.

You can smile to hide evil thoughts. You can steady your shaking hands and you can win someone over with the proper amount of charm slathered on. But the eyes – they are, truly, the windows into the blackest of black souls. They cannot be encouraged to mask the uncanny truths lurking inside even the craftiest human.

Her eyes threaten to give her away – and what I see in them is something that makes me shudder, something that makes me want to cower underneath the table until she leaves.

I do nothing of the sort, though, ignoring the chill in my blood, shaking aside the fear.

Her wild eyes study me from across the table as she sips her tea, her shaking hands carefully lifting the mug to her perfectly wide lips. I command myself to calm down. What could I possibly have to be afraid of?

Amos rubs my legs now, meowing, before rubbing hers. She reaches down to pet the cat.

And then, the devil cat does something he knows better than to do. He rushes over to the door off the kitchen, the one on the back wall. I wince. He knows better than to go near the door. He's not allowed over there.

I yell at him, 'Amos, no!' How *dare* he go near there. Fury bubbles inside. We ignore the door. We do not go near that god-awful door.

The hideous creature doesn't listen to my yelling. He ignores all reason and rules. Instead, he raises a paw to claw the door as if in an act of open rebellion.

Jane is on it, though. She rushes over.

'Amos, darling, what's in there? Do you need to go in there?' She reaches for the doorknob.

Suddenly, the will to move fast is back, and my legs listen.

I leap from my seat, bellowing, 'Stop!'

She turns to me, a hand on the doorknob.

I rush over, yanking her by her wrist.

She gasps as I tighten my grip on her.

'What are you doing?' I scream, inches from her face. 'What do you think you're doing?'

Stunned, she tries to say something, but she can't get out any words.

'We don't go in there. We don't. We *don't*,' I spew out, tears coming to my eyes. My heart races so fast, I think this might be it. This might be where I die, where my heart explodes, a bloody burst of fears, regrets and organs.

'I didn't know,' she retorts. No apology, no concern. She says it with a nonchalance, like she's talking about the weather or about the oil in the car or about a dirty dish.

'Don't touch it. *Get away, now*!' I demand, not caring that the moment is ruined, not worried about niceties. My whole body vibrates with uncontrollable anger, every muscle in my body tensed for a fight.

She could've ruined everything. She could've undone so much. How dare she come in here with those wild eyes and try to ruin it all.

'I'm leaving now,' she practically spits at me. She yanks her wrist back, and I reluctantly let go, ready to pounce on her if she reaches towards the door again.

64

I can barely see her through my blurry eyes, the tears welling. I swipe at my face, my breath shallow and fast.

Amos meows at me, sitting near the door. I lean on the stove, almost burning my hand. I pull it away fast.

She slinks away, out of view. I don't take my eyes from the door, still staring at the familiar knob even though the tears are fogging my vision.

The front door clicks. She's gone.

'Stupid cat,' I yell, and Amos puts his ears back, meowing as he dashes to another room.

The stupid cat almost did it. He almost did it, indeed.

Chapter 8

I turn the tap on the bathtub as I carefully step over the ledge, a feat I know I won't be able to do much longer. I'm actually quite impressed with myself that I can pull it off. This old woman's still got some miles left in her, I guess.

The hot water shockingly scalds my cold toes. I want to leap out, but I don't want to slip. Wet feet on a tile floor aren't a good mix. I endure like I always do, my feet blazing. I always make the water too hot.

After the burning sensation has settled to a bearable level, I judiciously lower myself down, clinging desperately to the sides of the claw-foot tub. I don't want to fall. A broken hip now and I'm a goner. I'll shrivel up in the water until I either die from starvation or from being waterlogged. Or I'd have to drown myself to put an end to the misery.

I always thought drowning would be a terrible way to go.

Such morbid thoughts, I chide myself. These are the thoughts of a frighteningly dark person, ones that won't do in old age. In truth, I guess I always had a little bit of a penchant for melancholy.

I lean my head against the ledge of the tub, the pockmark from the chip that's been there for decades settling against my neck. I stare up at the familiar ceiling, the dusty cobweb in the corner taunting me. How long ago did it take root up there? No matter. It's not like I can get to it anyway. It will live another day.

I settle my feet against the other end of the tub, thinking about what it would feel like to perish here. The chill of the water as it got colder and colder. The feel of my skin wrinkling, pruning from the waterlog. The endless moments of starvation, of pain, of wanting it all to be over. The harsh reality of being alone, all alone, in the final moments, something that's always near to my fears.

I sigh, shaking my head.

Yes, Mom always did accuse me of being a dark child, a shadowy character. Maybe that's why things turned out the way they did. Maybe that's why it happened. She should've known better than to push me, I suppose.

Then again, knowing limitations was never Mom's thing. Neither was justice. Or maybe she was right and I was just too sinister to tend to.

Maybe if my child were that way, I'd have done the same thing. Of course, I never had the chance to find out, a harsh reality I've faced over and over in the past decades.

In reality, I suppose I wasn't the most typical of little girls growing up. I was the girl caught torturing a dying bird in the corner of the school playground while my sister and her friends jumped rope. I was the girl fascinated by hell after a sermon at church, wondering how Satan chose his cronies. I was the girl drawn to blood in an accident when the other little girls averted their eyes. I was the girl who played with knives instead of dolls, who hid them under her pillow just in case.

I wasn't like the other girls, it's true. I wasn't normal, I suppose. Then again, what's normal? And I turned out okay, didn't I?

I sigh at the thought, childhood memories I've shoved aside for so long. Mother always told me I was the black sheep of the family. Looking back, she was sort of right. That used to bother me. Now, I'm used to it. And really, can you still be the black sheep if you're the only one? What does it matter at this point? It all turned out the same anyway.

Maybe my murky thoughts today are understandable, though. Maybe they have a lot to do with yesterday, with what nearly happened.

I've almost forgiven Amos.

I've almost forgiven her.

She didn't know. She couldn't know.

Still, who does she think she is, wandering about to and fro in my house, touching things that aren't hers? What kind of woman just goes about as if she owns the place? Sure, we were becoming – friends? I don't know – but still. There are boundaries.

She's pushed them. I don't like boundaries being pushed.

I settle into the hot water, relaxing into it, my creaking joints almost sighing audibly at the feel of the water surrounding them. It's been too long since I've afforded myself this luxury. I don't know why. It's not like I have anything else to do. Who cares if a bath takes a long time? What else can I do?

I open my eyes, staring at the ceiling again, the swirls always lulling me into a peaceful state. Today, though, staring upward, I feel reminiscent. Sometimes, I don't want to remember. It's too painful to think of all those other times in life when I wasn't lonely, when life was so different. It's hard to think back to the freedom when now I just feel suffocated and trapped. The window is my only outlet to the real world, and even it dims in comparison to my life experiences.

However, the mind is a curious thing, and despite the fact I know it'll throw me into a fit of sadness, it takes me wondering back now. Like a time machine, my brain escorts me to a segment of my life when I wasn't so lonely, a time when I wasn't the black sheep or a lonely widow. I return to a time when I was on the verge of excitement and newness. It was a moment when it felt like life was opening up instead of closing in on me, a time when a big bathtub and hot water weren't my greatest excitements.

A time when he was mine.

* * *

My coat wrapped snugly around me, I nestled into my scarf a little tighter as the January air bit into my face. I smoothed together my lips, hoping to redistribute the lipstick after the kiss we shared under the starlit sky.

'Beautiful night, huh?' he said, his silky-smooth voice enveloping me, making me feel at ease.

'A cold night, but beautiful,' I admitted as he grasped my hand, leading me down the street towards our favourite restaurant.

'Just like the woman I'm with,' he replied, and I felt my cheeks warm, my lips turning up into a smile. Just a few simple words, and I was putty in his hands.

We'd been dating for two months at that point, and I felt ... different. He made me feel real, made me feel like life was beautiful. In a family where I was often labelled as the odd one and so frequently pushed to the outskirts, he made me feel special.

He made me feel worthy. He made me feel like his number one. He made me feel like life could go somewhere, my hand in his. Most of all, he made me feel like the past – that thing I didn't want to talk about – didn't matter. None of it mattered with him. I would be better with him.

I never wanted to be owned by a man, by anyone really. I didn't want my heart to be his and his alone. Then again, I never thought I could be loved like that. I never knew I could actually let love in. But he made me feel otherwise. Those dark eyes, that smile, the sensation of his hand on mine. It gave me hope. It made me think life with him could be different, could be magical, could be beautiful. We could make something of this life, turn it into something grand. Being with him, I could be someone else.

When I saw him, I saw a future, a family, happiness. And when he saw me, he didn't see my shortcomings – which there were many of – he saw me, pure me, and apparently he liked it because he hadn't stopped coming around since that first night.

'I have a surprise for you. I hope you like it,' he murmured as he opened the door to Jack's, our favourite restaurant. He smoothed back his hair, a gesture I'd come to learn over the past months. It was his nervous gesture. I liked that I made him a little nervous.

'Oh, yeah? I hope it's that cheesecake they took off the menu. Did you talk them into putting it back on?'

'It's better than cheesecake,' he promised, leading me to our booth, our usual table, as the waiter came over to take our order.

Thirty minutes later I learned that the surprise wasn't cheesecake.

It was forever.

'I love you. Since the first time I saw you, your heart reached *out and grabbed mine. I think I can see forever with you. You make me more confident, more happy, more me. Will you be mine forever? Will you see where this life goes? Will you marry me?' His words caressed me from across the table, wrapped themselves around my brittle heart.*

Tears formed in my eyes and I smiled wider than I thought I ever could.

Down on one knee, this gentle, sweet man was pledging his life to me. And I found myself saying 'yes' without thinking.

I said yes to him, to the life we could have, and to the hope that it would be the start of a changed forever, one I never imagined was possible.

* * *

The water is chilling, as my toes tap on the side of the tub. My eyes are wet, but I honestly don't know if it's from the bathwater or from the memory.

So long ago. Who was I? Where is that woman with those luscious curls, tight breasts, smooth hands and hope in her eyes now?

I think about that sweet start, the feelings of forever and possibility swirling in my chest. I was happy once. I've almost forgotten that over the years, forgotten how happy I was with him that night. I've forgotten how he reminded me that I *could* be happy. I wish I could just go back, live in that moment forever. Such peaceful, optimistic thoughts that day brought.

It's good to remember, but it stings too. The pain of what can never be again is almost too much to bear. It weighs on my chest, seizing everything inside with a grasp so tight, it threatens to strangle me. Things could've been so different.

Why weren't things different? And how could life take such a sharp detour from what I pictured that night at Jack's?

I squeeze my eyes shut, trying to block out the sad montage that's destined to play – all the moments and smiles and hardships. If only I'd known then what I know now – if only I could've shaken that girl, lost in the promise of love and happiness. If only I could've warned her that life wasn't made on cheesecake promises.

I was too wise, too aware of life's harsh realities even then to naively believe everything could be happiness. How had I had been so foolish? Maybe I just needed an escape, starved for love, acceptance and forgiveness.

I had things I needed to make up for. I thought he would be the chance to do that. He would be the opportunity I needed to start over, to right so many wrongs and to find fulfilment I hadn't uncovered. For a short period of time, I saw myself as he did. I could see a person destined for a life of happiness instead of the person I used to be.

I saw a goodness in myself that he had recognised and brought out.

If only I could've hung on to that version of myself. There are so many if onlys.

I open my eyes, willing the montage of regret to stop. I stare at the water in the tub, thinking about how hard life is. Thinking about how hard getting old is. Thinking about how much I miss that couple, that girl I was once.

But there's no going back, not really. What's done is done, what's been lived has been lived.

Chapter 9

I think it's a few days after the door incident when she returns. I – like I so often do – lose track of time, of the days. When you're my age, every day is so similar that it hardly feels like there's a point to distinguish between them. They run into each other, every wakeup like the one before. Calendars become arbitrary when no one is expecting you anywhere. The days just meld into one giant string of moments of survival.

I'm getting the mail, a few advertisements for places I don't visit and the water bill, when I see her emerge from 312 Bristol Lane. She's wrapped in a hat, scarf and coat, an early-season frost having settled on the ground.

I study her from the crack in the door, wondering if she's over what happened. Wondering if she can move on.

She tentatively lifts an arm and then offers a wave and just the hint of a smile. I do the same.

We stare a long moment as if contemplating who will make the first step. It's her. She pulls her door shut and ambles down her steps, crossing the distance between our houses with ease. I wordlessly gawk at her, mail in my hand, as she bounds up the stairs on my porch and stands before me.

'Hi.' Her eyes pierce mine.

'Hi,' I reply, the soft word a whisper off my lips.

Once more we stare, not sure who will give in. This time, it's me.

'I'm sorry. I just ...'

'It's okay. You don't have to explain. But wow, it's cold. I could use some tea.'

'Me too.'

And with that, I turn, leading the way into the kitchen and our old habits, pleased that we are able to move past the awkward encounter and stubbornness.

Because I could sure use a cup of tea, and, in truth, I could use company.

We settle into our routine, the shut door lingering in the corner of the kitchen like an elephant. Somehow, though, we both manage to ignore it.

'So, anything new?' I ask as she puts the water on, opening the teabags but not yet putting them in the perfectly lined-up mugs.

She shrugs. 'Same old.'

'Boy, don't I know about that,' I mutter.

A silence lingers between us, one filled with tension. Things aren't smoothed over between us, not really. Perhaps it's my fault. There's still a deafening anger settled in my chest over what could have happened. Maybe it's irrational after all this time. Maybe it's ridiculous to blame her.

But I can't help it.

I lean on my hand, my head propped up on the kitchen table. She leans on the counter, her wrists delicately bent as she stands, staring at me, waiting for the kettle to come to a boil.

'I don't know that I've ever asked what your husband does,' I say, trying to make conversation.

'He works a desk job. Pretty much just a yes-man, you know. Running errands, all that.' She says it in an unimpressed tone.

'Well, that sounds like good work.'

She shrugs. 'He's no CEO or anything.'

'Does he need to be? I mean, being a CEO comes with a lot of responsibility. And requires a lot of time.'

'Yeah, I suppose. But it also comes with a lot of power. I always thought if I had worked somewhere, I'd want to be at the top. To know what that power feels like. It must be something, knowing you're in charge, knowing people respect you.'

There's a twinkle in her eye, and I realise, if given the chance, she'd be a real go-getter. She'd be ambitious to the point of self-destruction, perhaps.

'Did you ever think about working?' I ask, genuinely curious.

She shrugs. 'I have. But, well, I don't always do well with people.'

I blink, surprised by her response. 'Really?'

'Really. I'm a different person out there.' I assume she's referring to the world, society. 'Always have been. Here, I rein it in a little bit.'

I see a sadness on her face, a nuance I have yet to detect. 'Well, sometimes out there is overrated, huh? But I don't know, sometimes being inside isn't all perfect either. Life is hard.'

'Truth in that statement,' she admits, and the kettle begins to boil.

She reaches for it, her face stern. Perhaps I've said too much. Maybe I should've chosen better words but it's done now. She pours in the hot water, then carefully executes the dance of teabags and spoons as she so often has.

She turns and is walking towards the table, slowly.

I don't know whether she wasn't focused or if her hand was just unsteady. Regardless, before she makes it to the table, catastrophe strikes. The cup in her left hand shatters to the floor, hot water splashing and bits of the mug scattering everywhere.

'Oh dear,' I say, springing up to assess the situation, my bones screaming at me as I do, to help her. The popping sensation in my hip tells me it was a mistake, but there's no time to deal with that now.

She freezes for a moment, staring at the broken mug and the spilled tea.

'Shit,' she screams, and her face contorts.

'Are you hurt?' I study her hands, her legs, to see if there's blood. It looks like a bit of glass has sliced her ankle, blood trickling down and mixing with the tea and the mug fragments. 'Let me help,' I say, rushing over but not sure where to start.

Tears are now flowing down her face and her body shudders.

'There, there. It's fine. It's going to be fine,' I say because, in reality, it is. Nothing a bandage, some peroxide and a mop can't handle.

She sinks to the ground, finding a dry patch of floor to rest on. She pulls her knees to her chest and rocks, the tears falling wildly now, her sobs racking her body. I step around the puddle towards her, careful not to slip, but she holds up an arm, telling me to keep my distance. I'm not sure what's going on, truthfully. It's obvious to me, though, that the mug's not the most important thing that's broken today.

I back against the counter, staring at the tea, the blood, the shattered fragments on the floor. It strikes me how the pattern is so intricate, how it looks almost like an abstract painting. It's a beautiful mess, just like Jane. A beautiful mess indeed.

She continues to rock and sob as I head to the cleaning closet, her incoherent chanting sounding like a religious rite of the most sinister variety. Calmly, I find a mop and bucket. No use comforting her – you can't comfort those who don't want comfort, who won't listen to reason.

I mop up around her, tired from the labour but energised by the excitement.

A little blood never did scare me.

Chapter 10

'Mommy, please, please, please, please, please—' a voice shrieks beside the candy bars as I wait in line. The whiny mewl belongs to a little boy, about five, who is hanging off his mother's pants. I lean on my cart, winded from my walk up and down the aisles. The voice grates on my nerves, like nails on a chalkboard. I always thought the annoyances of humanity were much worse than any inanimate sound could be.

When I left the house this morning, I was bright and cheerful. I needed to get out of the stagnant house. I needed to stop feeling entombed by the walls. Despite the exhaustion in my weary bones, I told myself it's so good to be out and about around civilization, even for a moment.

Now, the hustle and bustle of Mark's Mart reminds me why sometimes staying put is better. It reminds me why, like Jane suggested, out there isn't so great.

'I'm sorry,' the woman says to me, and I shake my head.

'It's fine. It's a tough age, I imagine.'

'You have no idea.'

I take a deep breath. Words like these used to break me, but now they just cut like a dull knife. They remind me I've missed that window – not like I could've forgotten. Life is what it is at this point. No use worrying about it.

Except I know that's a lie. How can I not think about what I'm missing when I'm in that dusty house, day in and day out? How can I not mourn for what wasn't and what will never be? So many moments, memories were destroyed before they even had the chance to happen. I've missed out on so much, in truth, no matter what lies I tell myself.

When it's finally my turn at the checkout, I unload my cans of cat food for Amos, some tea and some other odds and ends to get me through. I don't eat much anymore, mostly because I'm not hungry but also because cooking for myself seems like a wasted effort.

I miss those dinners, those simple meals for two. It's one of the things I never really realised was so important – having someone across the table with you, sharing a meal. It's something I really miss.

The checkout assistant is a woman I don't recognise. She doesn't smile or ask how I am. I hate feeling like an old, cantankerous woman, but still where's the socialisation? Where's the care and concern? It seems like not that long ago, you'd be greeted with warmth in a situation like this. It felt like everyone in this town knew everyone and, more than that, wanted to know everyone. Not that I was ever one of those block party, bonfires-on-the-corner kind of women. I mostly kept to myself, even in my younger days. I was an outskirt sitter. But even from the outskirts, I knew the town was welcoming. Friendly. Warm. Now, the world feels a little cold. I don't like it. I miss the cordiality. I miss the good old days, even if they weren't so good in retrospect.

I guess that's the hell of getting old – always longing for what was and what can never be. Always living in two worlds: this world and the one you conjure up based on memories.

It's the fact that you're always wanting, in truth – whether it's companionship, health, freedom or any of the other multitude of things that you lose when you age.

I hand over the cash once the woman blurts out my total, not even bothering to look up from the machine in front of her. She doesn't even see me, and I'm standing right in front of her. She grabs the cash from me with a quick motion, shaking her head as she opens the drawer and huffily counts out change. Too bad. I'm a firm believer in using cold, hard cash. I don't believe in those newfangled cards and machines. Cash is familiar. It's the one familiar I still can cling to.

After instructing the bagging boy to put Amos's cat food in a separate paper bag – how dare he think he can just shove it in with all my stuff to flatten it – I look around for my trusted friend, the one who always chats with me, always helps me to my car.

'Where's the young man, the one with the blond hair and the earring?' I ask. It's a shame I don't know his name.

The assistant finally looks up, staring at me like the wretched witch she is. She almost sniggers at my comment, holding back an eye roll. 'You might want to be more specific.'

'The one who is always here on Thursday afternoons, who helps me to my car. You know, the earring, the deep voice?'

Her lips smack together and she looks heavenwards as if she'll see the answer written on the ceiling. What a dumb woman. I won't go through her checkout from now on just out of principle.

'Doesn't ring a bell. Josh, here, is the only bagger we have on Thursdays.' She gestures towards the lanky, dark-haired boy who almost put Amos's food in with mine. I study him, knowing I wouldn't trust him to put a single bag in my car. He looks shady, suspicious.

'No, the other one always helps me to my car. There's another boy who bags groceries,' I retort, but the woman shakes her head.

'Well, you must've imagined him then, lady.'

I grip the handle on the cart firmly as I glare at the witch of a woman. How dare she insinuate I don't know what I'm talking about. Of course there's another boy who works here. Of course there is. He always helps me to my car ... doesn't he?

I clench the cart even tighter, afraid I might bust the plastic piece with the mart's name on it. I know I'm not crazy. That boy – oh, I do wish I knew his name – always has a conversation with me too about— I don't really know right now. Something. We talk, yes we definitely talk about something. But he helps me with a smile, and I toot my horn when I pull out, and he waves. I'm sure he does, doesn't he?

My hands tremble from the effort as I slowly trudge forward, away from the horrible woman on checkout lane three and the lanky, creepy teen the woman tried to convince me is the only bagger. I feel a headache coming on. Stupid woman. She probably is just clueless. But why does she have me so upset?

Am I going crazy? Is she right? What's happening to me?

I tell myself to get a grip, that it's okay. It doesn't even matter. I don't need help anyway. I'm fine by myself.

I load the groceries in my car, the quiet task aggravating me. Each bag feels like a lead weight. I heave them into the car, my arms aching afterward. I get the task done, though. That's what matters. It's fine, all fine. I can still handle things myself. I sometimes look forward to these outings, the sheer idea of seeing people and being around them making me happy, making me not so lonely. But out here, I realise that maybe life at home isn't so bad. There, I don't have to put on appearances. I don't have to fake smile and tell the mother of an annoying brat it's all okay. I don't have to paint on a socially acceptable persona. I can shred that persona and just be myself, lost in the world I control.

I like that feeling of control, a feeling I don't sense here.

Plus, things have changed. I'm not really alone anymore. Jane has changed everything a bit. I'm not so disconnected. There really is no need to come out into the world anymore except for the necessities. I don't need to find companionship because there's a sense of camaraderie and excitement gained from just glancing through the window. It's my lifeline. My lifeblood.

And so I climb into my car, letting the cart roll where it will. I start the car and head home, back to the lane where I've lived for so long to settle in, to watch more unfold.

Suddenly, there's life on Bristol Lane again, and it feels so good. Even if I'm only a spectator.

* * *

With my arms tired from the taxing chore of loading the groceries in my car, I can barely make it through the process of carrying the bags into the house. I want to just flop into bed once I've made it to the kitchen, Amos meowing at my feet. I don't, though. I have to muster up some energy to get the groceries unpacked.

I systematically unpack the bags, stowing each familiar item in its designated spot in the fridge or pantry. I've got the unpacking process practically memorised, making it a mindless task. The only new addition to my grocery bags this week is a different kind of tea. I thought maybe it would be nice to give Jane a choice when she comes back over.

When I've finally finished the task, my bones aching, I stumble to the rocking chair. I'm too tired to even bother with tea. It's early evening now, the sun sinking lower and lower. How long was I gone? The trips to the store seem to take longer and longer these days. And they also claim more of my energy every week. What will I do if I can't muster up the strength for these trips anymore? How will I manage? I try not to think about it all. These are thoughts that scare me if I think too long. These are the times when the fact I have no one, no children or grandchildren to check on me, become starkly apparent.

I lean back in the chair, willing myself to stay calm. I'm fine. I still manage just fine. I've never been one to let anything or anyone get the best of me. I'm not about to start in old age. I've still got tenacity in me. I'll see this whole thing through, I will.

Looking across the street, I don't see Jane. That's a shame. I could use a good studying session today after the store trip sucked the life right out of me. I wish I could see her today, doing something, anything. What a bummer that they're in another part of the house now.

With nothing but grass and the shell of the house to look at, I rock gently, back and forth, lulling myself into a peaceful state of nothingness. My mind blank, I continue to rock back and forth. I feel Amos jump on my lap, and I stroke his soft fur gently, still rocking.

And then, I drift away, into that most peaceful place where real life can't get to me.

* * *

My heart pounds as I startle awake, grabbing the armrest of the chair. The gut-wrenching bark of a dog echoes off the house, a sound that's always sent terror right through me.

Eyes peeled open, I look out my window into the yard. Night has fallen, my rest apparently lasting longer than I thought it would. It's pitch black outside, the moonlight the only thing illuminating the horrifying sight before me.

The dog is a goliath of an animal, its mangy fur not detracting from its terrifyingly muscular build. It's the biggest dog I've ever seen, and its muzzle is covered in a frothing foam that screams illness. I clutch at my chest, the terror bubbling to an uncontrollable level. I can't speak, can't scream, can't move. Ice trickles through my veins, my skin freezing cold. Amos, back hunched, stands below my chair, hissing and growling in ways I've never heard from him.

I know reasonably the dog can't get to me, but it doesn't matter. The sight takes me back, throws me into a place of panic and of weakness. I don't like it one bit.

The horrifying mutt skulks through the yard, circling as if in wait of prey. It turns its head, and when it looks through my window, teeth bared, I'm convinced it wants to do me harm.

Tears well, and I bite my lip so hard to keep myself from screaming out. I clutch my left hand in my right, squeezing it so hard I think I might break it. My thumb rubs back and forth over the familiar scar, and I can feel a surge of pain so strong, I think there must be blood spurting from my hand. I think for a moment I'm going to look down and see the open wound, the red liquid gushing down onto the floor.

I tear my gaze from the vile creature to examine my hand, slowly peeling my right hand away, my breath laborious and my eyes stinging.

But there is no blood, no gushing wound. *Of course there isn't, you silly woman. Why would there be?* I'm truly going mad. I am.

I look at the scar that I haven't stopped to consider for quite some time. It's faded with age, blended into the wrinkly texture of a hand with skin that has seen the work of ageing. But the thin line is still there, and more than that, the memories are, too.

I find the courage to peel my eyes away from my hand and to peer back out into the darkness, terrified for a split second that the dog will have its frothing muzzle to the window, its jagged teeth snapping at the glass in an aggressive display of its power.

But when my eyes peruse the yard, they find nothing, not a single sign of the loose beast. It's gone, faded right into the night with the nightmarish memories from my past.

Where did it go? Will it be back? I can't help but wonder, worry, that I'll see it again.

Moments pass, and my heart rate slows to a normal pace. My head clears, and I take a few breaths. Amos is curled up, soundly asleep on the floor in the kitchen. That was fast, silly cat. Apparently the barking dog didn't make a huge impression on him.

I stare into the inky blackness for a while, the moon still shining in the sky. I think for a long while about the old memories, the old fears. I think about the sight of this mangy mutt that has brought it all back.

Some fears, some terrors last much longer than they should. Then again, maybe that isn't always a bad thing.

I peel myself from my chair, dragging myself to bed. It's a long walk up the stairs, my body still exhausted from the exertion at the store. I climb into bed in my clothes, too achy to think about changing.

I tuck myself under the covers, lying on my back as I often do. Before falling asleep again, my right hand finds my left, and I trace the scar once more, just to assure myself it's real.

I trace it gently back and forth, back and forth, until sleep claims me once more.

Chapter 11

So often in life, we mistakenly think that change is going to ease in, announce its presence and let us get accustomed to it.

I haven't mastered life, even at my age, but I've come to learn this: change is never easy, and it almost never gives a warning. One day, you're floating along, thinking all is well, and then the next, like a slap in the face, it's all irrevocably changed. You're left sitting in the dust, wondering how you missed it coming.

It's like that for 312 Bristol Lane.

For weeks, things appear great again. The July couple carries through, and I am almost envious of their affection. They're so smiley, so happy. She's like the sunshine-yellow dress – the perfect wife. They have a perfect home and they're the perfect couple. She visits me several times, and we sip tea on the front porch, the 'door day' and the 'broken mug day' seeming like they were just dreams. All is well, or at least I think so.

Of course, looking back, there were warning signs. Flickers of who she was hiding, what *they* were hiding. I just didn't want to see. Maybe I didn't want the fantasy world I'd created to disappear. Maybe I wanted to keep believing their love story was perfect, would be my comfortable company for my final years. Maybe I hoped it would remind me of my own early love story, of that swooning feeling, of those first-kiss moments. Maybe I just missed him, and I was soothing that pain by watching them.

Whatever it was, I know this – things are changing.

They're changing.

They're breaking.

I think it started as tiny cracks, almost unnoticeable signals of them coming undone. The angry gesture on the front porch over some argument I couldn't hear, smoothed over by a kiss on the cheek and what looked like an apology. Abandoned dinner one night in the kitchen, a screaming match ensuing as she stormed out ... followed by a sweet, tender embrace at breakfast the next morning.

I thought they were running their course, fighting like couples do. I thought maybe the honeymoon years were just wearing off because we all know they *do* wear off.

I thought they were okay. Maybe they thought that too.

But as the weeks go on, I realise something I hadn't before.

Something's not right. Something's not right at all. In fact, something's so grotesquely wrong and hideously tainted, I don't know if there will be any turning back.

Things haven't been right for a while now, I'm starting to realise. Behind that bubbly smile, that sunshine yellow, she's not perfect. Not even close.

Why with all bright stories is there a monster, unseen, that festers beneath the boiling surface?

As the weather gets colder, the frost settling in, it's clear that maybe I didn't really know my neighbour from 312 Bristol Lane at all.

Clearly, clearly the broken mug, the breakdowns, the unwarranted tears – none of it was a dream at all. It was only the beginning of what was to come.

*   *   *

A thin blanket of snow smooths itself over the front lawn, over the road, over the steps of their place. I stroke Amos, wrapping the thicker blanket around the both of us as we rock, staring out the window. I can feel the cold air streaming from the window, thinking about how an inspector would probably say this old window should be replaced.

But I don't want to replace it. It feels ... special. I've spent so many hours here, right here with it. There's nothing wrong with the old sometimes. The new isn't always better.

With the cold weather settling in, I've been seeing less and less of the couple from 312 Bristol Lane. It seems like a routine has established itself.

Every morning, he leaves for work in their car, a tie straight as can be, a briefcase in his hand. She doesn't walk him to the door. She doesn't kiss him goodbye anymore.

At exactly 5.01 p.m., the car pulls in, he gets out and the door slams.

Around 6.00 p.m., dinner is placed on the dining room table.

There's no dancing. They sit across from each other, at either end of the table, the silence between them discernible from over here.

I want to scream.

What are they doing? Where are the dancing, kissing, smiling days? What happened to them? How did things change so much? I wish I knew what was happening so I could help, but something is very wrong. There's been a continental shift.

Not just with them. With us too.

Jane hasn't been over in weeks, probably a month. Has it really been a month? It's hard to tell. I lose track of time. But I know it's been a while, and I'm worried.

At first, I thought I did something to make her mad. I thought maybe she was upset over the broken mug or about how I handled it. I thought perhaps there was more than I understood. That I'd said something that I forgot. I racked my brain over and over, trying to pull back our conversations, trying to analyse every minute detail for the misstep.

I came up empty-handed.

I considered calling their phone, but I didn't want to be a bother. Plus, I don't even have their number. I told myself they were just busy. She was probably doing some organising or in the middle of a sewing project or whatever housewives did these days. Maybe she was painting a room, perhaps a nursery. Maybe they were expecting after all.

Still, it's been a long time. I haven't really seen much of her, not during the day, even though I've been watching the house. I see her every now and then, but not as much as usual. What is she doing in that house? She *never* leaves. I've watched and watched obsessively so I didn't miss it. I know, though, she hasn't left that place. It's worrisome, frighteningly so. It doesn't do to be cooped up. I'm one to know. A girl that age needs friends, needs to be social. I want to see her smile. I want to talk to her about soap operas and pie and all sorts of things.

I miss her, the smiling, sunshine-yellow her. But what can I do about it?

What an excuse. I'm old, but I'm still alive. I can do something, surely. So I decide to take things into my own hands.

I just came home from the store, another trip out into the world to remind me why being cooped up isn't so bad. I made it, though, the bagger boy helping me this time. The lanky one, the suspicious one. I was forced to go through that awful woman's checkout lane again since she was the only one open. She is still claiming the other bagger boy was never there. It makes me suspicious. I hope nothing bad happened to him. I hope he's okay.

I don't like the lanky bag boy. I kept one eye on him at all times. Who knows what kind of crazy thoughts are whirling in the head of a boy like that? He has dark eyes, eyes I don't trust. I clutched my purse close as he loaded the bags in my car. I hadn't really wanted help out to my car, but the devil at checkout lane three insisted. Probably a scam to steal money from me or to cover her tracks over the missing bagger boy. He'll probably show up on a milk carton next month – do they still put missing children on milk cartons? I don't even know.

Maybe the lady at checkout three was just trying to be helpful. I looked a little frazzled today. I feel it. Still, people are rarely invested in anything outside of their own interests, so I'm wary. She's not getting one over on me, though.

Anyway, I'm back now and I carefully unpack the ingredients for a rhubarb pie, her favourite. My favourite too.

It has been so long since my hands have made a pie by themselves. I don't really know if I can do it but I need to try.

It takes me a lot of time just to get started, let alone to make the thing. I sit down every fifteen minutes or so to take a break, my breath raspy to the point of concern. But I'm nothing if not tenacious. My husband used to say I was stubborn. Maybe that stubbornness pays off sometimes.

In considering it, I realise I'm stubborn as a mule – that's what he used to say in our early days when we used to joke around a lot. He thought it was cute then. Stubborn is good when you're making a pie, but I've learned that stubbornness has its downside, too.

Amos sits at my feet, watching the oven as the pie cooks. I would lean down to peek at it, to flip the trustworthy oven light and watch the pie bubble up, but it's hard to stoop down that low. I decide to let the old oven work its magic. You have to trust in some things, after all, and it's never let me down yet.

When the timer startles me and I gingerly pull the pie out, my back aching with the effort, I am a little disappointed. It is definitely not the best pie I've ever made. It wouldn't be winning any farm show awards. I consider slamming it into the waste bin or opening up the window and bailing it out for the birds or shredding it with a knife, chopping it into little pieces and feeding it to the garbage disposal. I feel frustrated. Why doesn't anything work out like it should? After a few deep breaths like I was taught so many years ago and counting to ten, I reconsider. The pie smells okay. And what was that saying about the thought and all that really mattering?

Whatever it is, I decide the pie will be a good enough gesture. Whatever's happening with my neighbour – and I am convinced I'm not imagining it – maybe a pie will help. There isn't much a pie can't help with. Plus, it'll be a good excuse for me to get close to the house, to do some snooping and maybe figure some things out. Maybe if I can just peek in the front window, I'll be able to see into their living room, see what she's up to.

As I watch the pie cool, I realise maybe my logic is a little faulty. There are many things, now that I think about it, that a pie cannot fix. Arthritis, a lost cat, diabetes, a hole in a roof – pies really don't fix all that much, in truth. This pie idea was probably a waste of time.

But the love that goes into the pie – that could maybe fix a broken person. At least make them feel noticed. Isn't that half the battle in life, to be noticed? To be appreciated?

Goodness, now I'm just rambling to myself. Those are the worst moments – when I realise I'm babbling incessantly in my own head. At least I'm not in the habit of talking out loud to myself. At least, I don't think I am.

I gather the pie after it cools and haphazardly cover it in foil. I'm a little nervous ... the steps to my house are a bit slippery. I'll have to be careful. It might take me a while to get there, but that's okay.

I trudge across the yard, my feet shuffling. I try my best to avoid the icy patches on the front step, in the grass. It's a dangerous trek, especially with my hands full, and halfway through, I want to give up.

But I don't give up, not on tasks like this. Not on tasks everyone says are impossible.

I'm out of breath when I get to their steps, but I clamber up them. I get to the landing and feel like this was a dumb idea, a wretched, stupid idea. What will I say?

I've been watching and noticed you're sad? You don't seem yourself. You don't visit the old hag next door anymore, so I came to you.

This was foolish, utterly foolish. I really need to find a

hobby. Maybe I should move myself to one of those facilities for old people. Maybe I could take up knitting there. But then I look back at the house, the two-storey. So many memories. Can I really just give that up? That's even sillier talk. It's home, like it or not, lonely or not. It will always be home. I can't escape it.

What to do now? What if she sees me standing here like a mad old woman? Or worse, what if she's busy?

Suddenly, I start to think about all the things she could be doing in there.

What if she's having an affair?

No, that can't be. I've never seen anyone else go in.

What if she's doing something illegal?

Like what? I respond to myself.

Drugs?

That seems highly unlikely.

More likely than not, I'm just being overly imaginative. Overly worrisome. She's probably just tired of the winter weather. Maybe she's sick. Maybe she just wants to be lazy. I've been through my lazy times in life. I surely can't judge.

I realise my fingers are aching with cold now, the joints cracking when I unfurl my left hand from around the pie. The wedding ring that is nestled in its familiar spot stings against my skin, colder than the rest of my hand thanks to the metal. I inhale the frigid air, and it feels sharp against my lungs. I cough a little, my body expelling a freezing breath.

I wish I were back home, looking out the window. Suddenly, this is all too much effort, and for what? Some woman I don't really know, a woman who clearly is someone with a few screws loose? I shouldn't be messing with fire, shouldn't be poking at it. I guess it's in my nature to meddle, though.

I imagine Amos on my rocking chair, looking sadly out the window at me. He's probably meowing, scratching at the glass, wanting me to come back. That cat does need me. What would he do if something awful happened to me out here? I should be getting back before I slip and fall.

I can see it now … that'll cheer her up, when she finds an old woman dead on her doorstep. I picture myself sprawled about on the steps, the snow falling on my back as I rasp for air, broken ribs impeding my breathing. I imagine what it will feel like, my lungs burning, as I take my last breath.

Talk about having the opposite of my intended effect – not sure a dead body is what she needs to see. So, I decide to do the best I can. I precariously lean down – a task in itself – and put the pie on the stoop. I think about knocking, but I'm so slow, she'd be at the door before I get down the steps. I don't want to embarrass her. I don't want to make things awkward. I just simply wanted to do something for a neighbour, to let her know people care. I want to prompt her to reach out, to confide in me. I want to know what's going on over here. I'm sure she'll know the pie's from me; she will. And then, if she wants to talk, she'll know my arms are open. I imagine her coming over for a cup of tea, filling me in and easing my mind. It's going to be okay. I'll make sure of it.

It's perfect really, even if the pie is frozen when she finds it.

It's the thought, remember?

Satisfied that I've come up with a workable solution, I wipe my hands, a little clapping noise occurring when they brush against each other.

'I'm coming, Amos,' I proclaim, glancing down the empty cul-de-sac road, finding it empty as usual. No surprise there.

It's always empty. Except for 312 Bristol Lane and me, and a few birds now and then.

I scuttle back home, treading cautiously over the slick spots. I open the front door and plop on the reclining chair once I'm inside. It was his favourite chair, and now I see why. Even after all these decades, it's cosy.

I take a few deep breaths, the cold easing itself out of my body, but not completely. I'm exhausted. I think I'll take a nap now. There's no harm in a nap. It's one of the perks of my current life status – no one can judge me for napping all the time. Plus, after that trek in the bitter cold, I've earned it, right?

I ease the recliner out, my coat still on, and lie back, looking at the ceiling. It isn't long until my eyes are closed and I feel myself drifting, drifting away. Sometimes I think the drifting part is nice, so nice. I'd like to just keep on drifting, you know?

Chapter 12

The first thing I notice is my neck.

Gosh, it's killing me. I swear it audibly creaks as I slowly come to, the darkness enveloping me in a way that scares me. Where am I? What am I doing here? It's so black, so dark. My heart catches a little. It's too dark.

It takes me more than a moment to remember. The older you get, the longer it takes.

That's right. The pie. Number 312 Bristol Lane. The long walk. The resting on the recliner.

I slowly sit up, my neck reminding me that sleeping on the chair is never a good idea. I take a deep breath before forcing myself to my aching feet. How long have I been asleep?

Amos meows at my feet as I stumble to the light switch in the living room and then the one in the kitchen. I flip it on and study the clock on the wall. It's seven p.m. I don't even remember what time I sat down on the chair. I don't really feel rested, though. Just groggy. That walk wasn't very long. How depressing that a single walk across the street exhausted me like that.

Suddenly, I worry that I missed everything. I stumble towards the window, ignoring my growling stomach. Their lights are on. I slump into the rocking chair, staring, trying to appraise the situation.

I don't see them at the table, but I've missed dinnertime. I glance to the porch. It's really dark and with this angle, I can't tell if the pie is still there. They must've gotten it, taken it in. I'm sure. But I didn't get a thank you. Maybe she doesn't know it was from me.

Then again, maybe I slept through her knocking. Who knows what happened. It's out of my hands now.

I still feel like maybe it was pointless. I exhausted myself for nothing ... and now I've missed so much. What a terrible plan.

Still, at least I tried. I study the empty room now, worrying and wondering. Where are they? What are they doing? Is she feeling better?

And that's when it happens.

Like an out-of-control freight train, I see him appear in the window, his hands waving fiercely as he stops by the table, leaning on it. His posture is tense, like he can't rest. He looks different. I can't figure it out. He's yelling, his mouth angry and wide.

And then she appears. She's talking – no, she's screaming with her hands. I can't make out the words. I try to read her lips, but it's all happening so, so fast. She's yelling, articulating with those hands. Her gestures are stabbing and pointed.

Their voices increase. She stomps towards him, and then she shoves him.

I cover my mouth, shaking my head. What is she doing?

At first, I think I'm mistaken. The shove I thought I saw can't be. That's not how they do things. That's not who they are. She's not like that. Sure, she has her issues, but she's not a physical person. This isn't her, not really. Yes, things have been changing, but I still don't think that's who they are. This isn't the woman who makes me tea and chats about soap operas. This isn't the woman in the sunshine-yellow dress. That's not her.

Is it?

But then it happens again. She shoves him a little harder this time. He's a small man, some would even call him frail. Sure, he's bigger than her, but there's this energy about her that makes her a force. Even from here, the way she rages like a rabid animal is terrifying. I can't imagine being up close.

He feels that force. He backs away. It looks like he's begging her to stop.

But she's out of control. Screaming, shrieking, clawing at him. Hitting him now. Punching him. More screams. More shrieks. More wild flailing, slamming him against the wall suddenly and violently throttling him. I bite my lip, feeling so helpless, as my fingers curl around the rocking chair handles. I want her to stop. I want all of this to stop. But what can I do? What can I *really* do? The devastating reality creeps into my veins, crawls under my skin, and settles in my chest.

I can't do anything.

He grabs her wrists and tries to contain her, but how do you contain someone so lost?

It's hard to watch, really. My stomach turns and churns, and I think I might be sick. I feel tears welling. *What's going on with her? Why is she doing this?*

She keeps screaming, and he no longer looks tense. He looks beaten. He looks broken. When he finally lets go of her wrists, she wildly thrashes a candlestick from the table at him before stomping off, the candlestick tossed to the ground.

And then it's quiet, just him, alone, standing for a long moment where he was. Eventually, his hands ruffling his hair, he moves dejectedly towards the window and stares out. His eyes peer off into the distance, at what, I don't know. He looks changed somehow, aged. My soul breaks for him. I hurt for him, almost as if I can feel his hurt through the window. Maybe I can, in some ways.

My heart's racing. What have I just witnessed? What's going on with them? Why is she so mad?

Questions, questions, questions, but never any answers. The window frustrates me today. It's not a place of solace or excitement or love. Today, it's a place of evil. It suffocates me, makes me think about how exasperating life is. The smiles have faded, and the sweet moments at 312 Bristol Lane have vanished without a trace.

They can get them back, I think to myself, breathing through the fear. I convince myself it's one fight. It's one bad, bad fight. She'll come to her senses. They'll work it out. There will be some profuse apologies tomorrow, a warm embrace, and they'll put this behind them. We all have things we need to put behind us.

Soon, they'll be back at that table, dancing to soft music and eating pot roast, laughing. She'll put on that sunshine-yellow dress and mosey over, thank me for the pie, laughing because she didn't realise it was from me. She'll tell me some ludicrous story about how they thought the pie was poison. She'll talk about losing her temper with him over a misunderstanding. An apology will ensue. She'll find her smile again. All will be well at 312 Bristol Lane, and I'll sip my tea, rocking and watching their love story continue.

This is just a rough patch. It is. I'm sure of it.

I watch for another moment, his miserable face threatening to waver my resolve, my confidence in their ability to fix things.

But I decide he deserves his privacy. He doesn't want someone watching this intimate moment; it can't be easy. I decide to give him that right, to let it go, to let him lick his wounds. He needs some space from her, from everyone. I can give him that. I might not be able to do much, but I can at least do that.

'Come on, Amos. Want some food?' I ask the cat. I know it's late and not really time to eat, but sometimes you just have to break the rules, you know? I open a second can of tuna delight for Amos, glopping it into the dish.

I usually don't have tea this late – it makes me have to pee in the middle of the night, plus the caffeine sometimes stirs me awake, tossing and turning in bed. It doesn't do for an old woman to be awake in the middle of the lonely night. It's hard on the mind, on the heart, thinking about the loneliness. There's no window-watching then. There's just me and the darkness. I prefer to sleep right through.

Something tells me, though, I'll be awake tonight anyway, lost in my thoughts and worries about those kids across the street – after all, they're still kids to me.

They need to work it out. She needs to find herself. I thought the pie would help, but it didn't.

I look at the stove and think to heck with it. I put on some water for tea, and then saunter over to the kitchen chair and stare at the blackness outside as I think about what this could all mean for 312 Bristol Lane – and for me as my daily watching has taken quite a turn for the worse.

After the screeching kettle alerts me that the water is hot

enough, I make my tea, careful to only fill it halfway, before trudging back to the rocking chair, deciding I need to take inventory before bed.

He's gone now, no longer staring into the blackness of the night, no longer visibly lost in thoughts and fears. I take a deep breath, feeling better.

The lights are out in the dining room and there's nothing to see. It's sort of a blessing to not have to stare at the dining room table devoid of a candlestick, or to peer at the wall where she had him pinned not very long ago. The darkness suits the dining room, covering up the hostile crimes committed there. It's blacking them out, allowing me to hang on to the tiny thread of hope I have that all can be fixed.

But then I see it.

The teacup in my two hands, the hot steam warming my face, I do a double take, almost not believing my eyes.

A figure in the darkness coming towards the dining room window at 312 Bristol Lane. Closer, closer, the frame comes into view. My heart thuds, my fingers chilled despite the steaming mug between them.

Jane stands, emotionless, staring out the window.

No, that's not quite right. She's not just staring out the window. She's glaring, her eyes burning wild with a rage only present in monsters of the darkest kind. And she's not just glaring at anything. She's not just aimlessly looking out the window, seething with whatever anger is inside her. It's scarier than that. Because, as I look out the window, I realise I'm not crazy. I'm not imagining things. She's glaring out the window and staring right at me.

She's mouthing something to me, but I can't make out the words.

Panic grips at my heart, and I think about calling the police. But what will they say? Who will they believe? I'll be locked away for sure, Jane convincing them I'm a mad old lady. Checkout lane three will certainly back that statement up. And then where will we all be? Where will he be, with no witness in this dusky house to keep an eye out?

I slowly stand, my pulse beating crazily as I turn my back on the window, my breathing rapid. I rush towards the counter to place my mug near the sink, spilling some tea on the way but not caring. There are bigger problems now. I breathe in and out, calming myself, telling myself there's nothing to fear.

But that's the thing about fear. Even when you try to tell yourself it's not there, it is, lurking in the corners of your being, playing on every worry and doubt you've ever had.

The tea keeps me up all night, but it's so much more than that.

Because, over and over, I replay the scene I witnessed. I replay the fear I felt. Most of all, I think about the sight of her glaring out that window, like she wanted to kill me. And over and over, all night, I try to decipher the words she mouthed to me, no answer coming to light.

Sleep doesn't come, only fits of questioning, periods of doubt, and endless nightmares, both fantasy and real.

In many ways, I suppose life has been a waking nightmare for me, and with this turn of events at 312 Bristol Lane, I shudder with the realisation that maybe the nightmare's just beginning.

Chapter 13

The new year. God, we need a new year, *I thought to myself as I sat, staring out my bedroom window into the murky blackness.*

I'd thought things would be different now that some time had passed. It felt like this year would be better. I would be better. I'd make Mom and Dad proud.

But everything had changed, and when families across the country were ringing in a new year, I sat in my room, alone, wondering if anything would be okay again.

I'd tried so hard to be good today. I'd made dinner for Mom and Dad. Mom refused to come out of her room, even when I'd gently knocked.

'Get the hell out,' she'd bellowed through snotty tears. Dad had stormed down the hallway like a bulldog, shooing me from the room.

'You little bitch, get moving. Get away. Are you a moron? Leave her alone. You've done enough.'

I'd rushed to my room, the meatloaf I'd carefully made rotting away on the kitchen table, just like everything else.

I deserve this, *I thought.* It is my fault. It's all my fault. *My arms wrapped around myself, I stared out the bedroom window,* looking at the starry sky, wondering how everything got so messed up, trying to sort it all out.

My chest hurt. Maybe it was guilt. Maybe it was grief. Maybe it was fear.

I didn't know at the time. It was too complicated.

She shouldn't have treated me like that, *I thought, the words dancing in my mind. I tried to shove them away, but they kept pounding against my brain.* She should have been nicer. She always pushed things.

I really hadn't meant for it to happen, the shove going a little too far. It hadn't been on purpose, just like I'd said.

But still, I'd done it. There was no denying it. I'd changed our lives forever.

Sitting, staring out the window, though, one thought developed. One ugly, sinister thought: it's just me now. There's no one else to compete with.

Chapter 14

This is why I have rules about tea.

I was up at least four times last night – twice to use the bathroom and twice because I jolted awake, the caffeine in my blood too much. I was restless, I was bored, I was lonely. I was dancing around in all sorts of memories I didn't want to think about.

The second time I awoke, around four in the morning, I decided enough was enough. What was the sense in pretending anymore? I got out of bed and wandered down the hall, thinking of heading to the kitchen to start the day, even if it meant staring out into the darkness.

I passed a few hours in the old recliner in the living room, rocking back and forth, telling myself I just wanted to sit somewhere comfortable.

In reality, I don't think I was ready to sit at the window with the darkness still present. If I was being honest with myself, I was afraid of what I might find lurking in the darkness, what I might witness. There are some things that make you anxious for daylight.

I think I dozed off, though, because when Amos's meows startle me awake, I'm still in the chair but it's now light. The night has passed, the long, horrifying night.

After slowly peeling myself from the recliner's comfortable grasp, I stretch, feeling quite rough but knowing I need to face my fears. Plus, I'll admit, I'm curious. How will they be today? Was last night all just a bad, nightmarish encounter that is smoothed over now? Are they back to normal? I need to figure it all out, no matter what.

I traipse to the kitchen, Amos still meowing, and I find a can of tuna to feed him. I plop the food into the bowl, noticing that although he rushes to his bowl, he somehow looks as frazzled as I'm feeling – or maybe it's my imagination. I really should brush that guy. His fur is looking a little bizarre.

I trudge to the front door, deciding to get my mail. Did I get the mail yesterday? I don't know. Is it too early for the mail now? I'm all confused, my messed-up sleep schedule throwing everything off. I feel really out of whack this morning.

I open the door, glancing over at 312 Bristol Lane, thinking about the scene from last night and shuddering. What happened? I wonder if everything is okay. I can't help but worry.

I reach into the mailbox, my hand feeling around and finding nothing. I must've gotten the mail or none came. Hard to tell. When did I last get the mail?

My inability to think coherent thoughts scares me. I need to get it together. It wouldn't do to go mad, it really wouldn't.

I'm ready to close the door and head back inside, to make some more tea and get myself awake, when I glance down.

There, sitting underneath the mailbox, is a foil-wrapped pie. It's familiar. Then I realise it's the pie from yesterday. She must've returned it.

What does that mean? Why would she do that?

I sigh in frustration, wondering why I even tried at all. Quickly, though, my frustration turns to something else.

Anger.

I crouch down to reclaim the pie, shaking my head in frustration. All that work, and for what? What good did it do? And how selfish can she be? I traipse back to the house, slamming the door shut behind me, a photograph in the entranceway shaking a little from the intensity.

I stomp across the entranceway and into the kitchen, finding the waste bin.

'Fine then. Be that way,' I bellow to the empty kitchen, slamming the pie into the bin, the foil cold to the touch. I wipe my hands, and Amos pauses from eating to look at me, probably wondering if he should dash under the sofa.

I lean on the counter, my breath ragged from exertion and from irritation. Some people just don't get it. Some people just can't appreciate anything. Maybe some people really aren't worth the effort, the time.

I know it's stupid. It was just a pie, for Pete's sake. It's not like it really was a grand gesture. But in many ways, it was. It was me trying to make amends – for what? Why am I involving myself so much in their lives? True, with them being the only other house on the lane, it's easy to get enveloped by them. Still, my attachment is probably unhealthy. I really should let it go, let them go about their business.

As I find my way over to my rocking chair, though, I know I just can't let it go. I can't just close my eyes and pretend it's not happening. It's just not in my nature.

* * *

I'm in a weird mood now. It's ten in the morning. He's gone to work – I saw him leave. Maybe it was my imagination, but his shoulders looked a little lower today. His head hung just a bit more towards the ground. His pants were a little wrinkled. He wasn't his crisp, bright-eyed self.

I get it, though, because neither am I.

I'm tired from last night's adventures – if you call the bathroom and an abandoned room an adventure, which I do these days. I'm still stewing from it all. It seems silly that the people living next door can affect my mood so readily. But they do. They can. They're in many ways my only human interaction, even if it is observational. Their lives, their story, creep around me like a bad weed that needs to be plucked. The weed, though, has blossomed, tricking onlookers into thinking it's a soft, spindly flower.

How long until the thorns on the weed prick me? How long until I have the strength to pluck the weed from the ground and throw it into the woodchipper until it disintegrates into unrecognisable flecks? Will I ever have that strength, or has the weed wrapped around me too closely, like a vine entangling me?

I rock back and forth, back and forth. Amos is fed. I have my cup of tea – half full but still sloshing dangerously close to the edge since I'm rocking. I'm feeling a little dull. I do wish she'd come over. I could use a visitor. Plus, I'm worried about her. Really worried.

I'm also, in honesty, scared. I want her to come over, yet I don't. It's that odd push and pull we feel so often in life. The wanting, and the not wanting. The needing and the fear.

I rock and rock, my mind a haze, unable to focus on a clear thought until, finally, there is nothing.

I must have drifted off because suddenly, my eyes are snapping open at the sound of a rapping at the door. I almost spill my tea, which is now lukewarm, as I spring up.

It has to be her. Jane from 312 Bristol Lane. She's come to her senses. Maybe she just needed to get some anger out. She's obviously feeling better.

I open the door, and there she is. Royal blue dress, the one from that night so long ago. Coat wrapped around her. A black scarf dramatically draped around her neck. I bite my lip, wondering what I should do. Part of me wants to slam the door. But a bigger part of me is curious, and I've never been one to say no to curiosity, even if it is of the dark kind.

'Hi,' she says, a weak smile telling me she's still in there. Relief cloaks me. Despite the pie situation and last night, I feel her weaselling her way back in. God, maybe I've become soft. Or maybe it's something else entirely. I don't have time for internal debates, though, because she's here, and I know I need to find out what's going on. I push down the creepy-crawly feeling on my skin and pull the door open a little wider.

'Come in,' I demand, ushering her out of the cold and into the kitchen. 'Can you stay a while? Can I put on some tea?' I ask, before inwardly chiding myself. Why am I being so friendly? I have a right to be a little peeved, after all.

'I've got it,' she says, ambling towards the kitchen like we haven't missed a beat, like last night didn't even happen.

She heads for the kettle and starts the water boiling as I take a seat. The exhaustion fades. It feels so good – so darn good – to have company. It feels good to see her out of that house, up and about.

She wordlessly gets cups ready, finds the teabags and gets out the sugar before sitting down with me.

'So what's new?' I ask once she's sitting across from me, wondering how to approach the subject.

She sighs, running a hand through her hair. 'I don't know, really. I'm sorry I haven't been over for a while. It's been so long, I know.'

I consider mentioning the pie, asking about it, but now, in the light of day with her here, it seems ... petty. Maybe the pie was just gross, or maybe she just didn't want it. What's it matter anyway? Am I really going to cause a drama over a pie?

Yes, yes, I would. But something tells me not today. Today isn't the day to start something. I know what she's capable of, and I'm not up for a fight, not right now. So I let it go.

'Don't apologise. I know how things can get. I'm glad to see you now.' And despite everything, it *is* true in an inexplicable way. I want to hate her, to want nothing to do with her. But somewhere inside of me, there's a happiness to see her. In spite of everything, in spite of the true side of her I've witnessed, and even in spite of the terror building, I'm glad to see her. A huge piece of me does want everything to be okay, for her to be okay. I want things to go back to how they were, our afternoon tea and gossip sessions. I want to see that smile, that steady, calm woman who moved in. I don't like the woman I saw a glimpse of last night, not one bit. 'Is everything okay?' I ask, treading cautiously.

'I don't know. I really don't know.'

I sit in silence, giving her space to breathe, to muster courage to say what she needs to say.

'Things are just ... different. I'm different.' In her voice is a tone I haven't sensed before. Maybe it's dejection, or maybe it's a moroseness on a whole other level than before. Whatever you label it as, it's clear that something's plaguing her, and that she's not the same. She is indeed different.

I consider saying I know. I want to tell her I saw her last night, saw her with him. I don't. That would be spectacularly creepy. I don't want to scare her off. Instead, I sit quietly, waiting for her to continue. She stares at her cup of tea, her fingers delicately touching the spoon she's placed on the table. She mindlessly traces the outline of it on the wooden tabletop, seemingly lost in her own world. I wonder what kind of world that truly is these days.

'I just ... I feel angry. Frustrated. Sad. It's hard to explain,' she continues.

I reach across and pat her hand. 'Life is hard, you know?'

'I know. But it's just ... I'm so frustrated.'

'About what?'

'I don't know. I know that's a terrible answer, but I really don't know the root of it. But mostly, it's him. He makes me so mad. He's so pathetic sometimes, you know? So weak and so ... just so weak. He's constantly working, constantly leaving me there in that house while he's out. And there's this secretary, Sheila. I know she's pretty. I just know it. And I think he might be cheating with her.' She stares at me now, her words no longer hesitant or morose. Instead, there's a fire fuelled by rage in her eyes and in the tone of her voice. Her words practically grate her throat as she spews them out, and once she's finished, I notice she's clenching her jaw.

I blink, the random slew of words causing me to pause. 'Honey, when would he be cheating? Doesn't he work a lot?' I stop myself from revealing the fact I've seen him come home every single day at the same time. He's practically never late, punctual as always. He never leaves at random hours, never disappears for long chunks of time. I don't mention this though; that is for me to know, to savour on my own. Still, she's not a fool. If I know he never disappears, she does too. Her accusations just don't make sense.

She lets out a little laugh. 'Men have their ways. It wouldn't surprise me. He never can say no to anything. Why would he say no to her? I'm sick of worrying about it. He's not getting away with it, you know? He can't even get me pregnant. He's sure as hell not going to go screwing around with other women, making a fool of me. I won't be second. I just won't be second.'

Her fists are clenched. I study her face. I see a bubbling fury up close, the kind I've only witnessed from the window before now. A rage the sunshine-yellow dress woman who moved in didn't seem to know, or at least was very good at masking.

The monster rears its ugly head.

But an anger like that, it's chilling, and it's not something that comes out of nowhere. It's not something you can just turn on. It must have been dormant all this time. It's the kind of inner demon you possess for a long while, covering faintly just so it can slip beneath the surface, toiling away until it's time to emerge. She must be good at smiling to cover herself.

I get it. I don't fault her. Life is brutal. We all wear the mask we have to wear to make it through.

'Is that what's really going on? Is it the baby situation? I know how rough that can be. I know what it's like to be disappointed every single month, to feel like you're lacking. It can play on a woman.'

Her fists are still clenching. She hisses her words through gritted teeth. 'It's probably because he's so worthless. It's because he's such a useless man. He refuses to go to the doctor. I bet he knows it's him. It's his fault.'

I take a deep breath, trying to figure out how to proceed. 'You know that's not fair. You know it. I think maybe, just maybe, you're hurting from all this and from something else from the past. I don't know. I can't be sure. But it seems to me like behind that anger is pain. But don't let yourself drown in it. It seems like you have a good man. Don't push him away. Don't hurt him because you're hurting. Let him love you. Let your love get you through.'

I hear my advice, the words of an old woman who has been alone a long time. In some ways, I don't have the right to tell her what to do. I know she'll do what she will anyway. Still, the words ring true, feel good to say aloud.

She stares at me, those lost eyes. So much pain. So much anger.

So much frightening vehemence.

I'm worried ... and not just for her.

For him.

The kettle screeches, and she jumps up, a grin on her face as she pours and changes the subject, chattering about the new character on the soap operas, about this new kind of tea she bought that I should try and about a pie recipe she found.

'Speaking of pie,' I begin when the opportunity arises, but I'm not sure how to proceed.

'Uh-huh,' she says as she sips on her tea.

I stare at her, hoping that I've lead her into a discussion of the pie, and more than that, I've given her an opening to discuss last night. I need to figure out what happened. It's all so confusing.

But I don't see any recognition in her face. She doesn't jump

119

in with an explanation for the returned pie or what happened. She doesn't say anything about last night. She just stares at me over her cup, an eyebrow raised. Her eyes practically laser into me, and I suddenly squirm under her gaze.

'Never mind,' I offer, waving a hand. I hate myself for letting it go, but what else can I do? I don't know what I expected. I guess a part of me hoped somehow there would be an explanation, a mitigation of what I witnessed. A part of me desired a wiping away of the sins of last night so that I could move on without trepidation. I could go back to my easy window-watching, the gorgeous moments between them brightening my days.

Instead, I'm left with the ugly truth that something is off, and I don't quite understand it. Perhaps it's the lack of understanding that irks me the most.

She stays for a while, and her pleasantness almost convinces me that I was crazy to think such dark things about her, even with last night still reverberating in my memory.

The woman before me who talks about the latest magazine article she read about yoga and the new oven she's picked out is a far cry from the rageful demon I saw last night. What's happening? What is going on? It's all just too much for me, it really is.

When she leaves, I see the bubbles of the old Jane shining through.

I tell myself she's just under a lot of pressure, that she's not all bad. It's a hard time they're going through. I've been through the infertility situation. I get it. It wears on you, especially as a woman. Thus, when I watch her cross the front yard and amble in through her front door, I hope things will change. I hope last night was a one-time occurrence. I hope she won't shatter my image of who she is or who they are together. I hope they can be different than what I fear they'll become. I hope she comes to her senses before he does and leaves.

Because, despite it all, despite those scary cracks I'm seeing in her, I think she's good deep down. I think, behind her bruised, battered, and tarnished heart, there's still good there.

There has to be good, because the alternative is too much to bear.

Chapter 15

The red-checked blanket beneath us, I stretched my long, pale legs out in the mild November sun. The rays warmed my body in a way that felt heavenly, not too hot and not too cold. His hand was on mine, and I was content, really content. I hadn't felt that way in a long, long time. Too long.

He had taken me away, an hour outside of town. It felt good to be away from Mother, always nagging me about my moods and my behaviour. You'd think a twenty-year-old would have some freedom, some space, but not from that woman. That woman would nag Jesus if she had a chance, I swear.

'Beautiful,' he said, leaning against me, his cologne wrapping itself around me. I took a deep breath, never wanting to forget the scent, to forget the feeling of sitting there in the middle of the park, alone in a sea of laughing families and screaming children.

With him, I felt alone – but in a good way. He soothed me.

A part of me wondered if I only liked him because he was so agreeable. He let me be my bossy self. He let me choose where we went and what we did. He never asked too many questions. He couldn't say no to me … but a girl deserves to be spoiled, doesn't she?

And he didn't seem to mind. I was the take-charge decision-

maker. He was the go-with-the-flow kind of guy. Opposites and all that.

We were good together.

From the time I saw him walk into that restaurant, his stiff-collared shirt contrasting starkly with his dark eyes, I knew there was something about him. I was drawn to him like an animal to prey. I had to devour him. I was starving for him before I even knew who he was.

But he was a gentle man, a man who took it easy. He languidly followed the path at his own pace.

Enough was enough.

'You know,' I said, looking into those dark eyes, 'I'm about tired of this.'

'What?' he asked, grinning.

'I'm tired of dating a man who has yet to kiss me. What, do you hate red lipstick or something?' I asked.

'Quite the opposite,' he replied, his hand rubbing mine. 'I was just waiting for the perfect moment.'

'Well, we're sitting on a picnic blanket on a beautiful afternoon. I'm wearing my best sundress and I feel like my hair is pretty good today. I can't think of a better time. It's been three weeks. Don't you think it's about time?'

'Do you ever just let things happen?' he asked, smiling.

'I'm not that kind of woman,' I replied, turning to him and leaning in, claiming his lips with mine.

It was a sweet kiss, the warm rays of the sun heightening the experience. The electricity jolted through me, the feel of his lips warming me even more.

It felt right. It felt so right.

The kiss intensified, his hand finding my cheek, his rough palms scratching against my face. I liked the feel of his hand on *me, turning my jaw just the right way. I liked how he was taking charge. I submitted to him just a little. It felt good to lose control, just for a moment. I felt safe enough with him to give in, to let go.*

'I think I love you,' he whispered into my lips when he pulled back.

'I know I love you,' I replied, never one to mince words. Because it was love, pure and clear. I loved that man. And for once in my life, I was positive that love was going to be a good thing.

* * *

How do the years fly by so quickly? In some ways, I can close my eyes and imagine the feel of the sun, the touch of his palm on my cheek. I can picture us laughing in the park, watching the little kids ride by on bicycles, their parents relaxing at their own picnic in the November sun. In other ways, it seems like a lifetime ago. I don't recognise those people, the wrinkly skin on my hands as I hold my cup of tea reminding me the day of smooth, soft hands is long gone. Days of sitting in the sun, of talking about kissing and love are gone. I miss those days so bad it hurts.

I'm eating a sandwich at the table, the silence of the house allowing me to revisit this scene. I'd forgotten about it for a while. Maybe it was intentional. Sometimes I think the human brain really is a wonder – it protects us from things that are too painful. It makes us forget even the beautiful moments so we don't have to endure the feelings of loss.

Today, though, the first kiss came swooshing back like the tap was on full tilt. The memory flooded into me, transporting

125

me back as I chewed on the stale bread in my turkey sandwich, throwing Amos a scrap.

How do you learn to live without those moments? How can life be so cruel? In one moment, you're kissing on a picnic blanket, life feeling perfect, and then, before you know it, you're a bag of bones at a table, alone, in the mausoleum of a life gone by.

Back then, I'd been a dumb girl who thought love could last forever, that life could last forever. We actually used to talk about rocking on the front porch together, hand in hand, our wrinkly skin and memories keeping each other company. I thought we'd grow old together. I never, ever pictured life like this – me in this house, alone, talking to a cat.

Old age is much worse than anyone could prepare me for. It's much sadder, emptier, darker. It's hard to find happiness. More than that, it's hard to hold on to happiness, my desperate, pawing hands never fast enough to clutch it before it crashes to the ground. Still, I have no choice but to try. I'm still breathing, and while I'm still breathing, I'm still living, like it or not. I've got to find something to live for, no matter how small.

My plate clatters as I drop it in the sink, too tired to deal with running water for one dish. What does it matter? I never liked doing dishes. I hated, day in and day out, washing up like a servant. The laundry. The cleaning. There were so many days it was all too much. Maybe it's penance or due justice that, now, I have no one to do dishes for, laundry for, but myself.

I stumble over to my seat, to my cordless television that's way better than any story on the real television. It's sunny, the bright light gleaming off the snow and burning my eyes. I'm too lazy to find sunglasses. They look silly on me anyway. I always thought they accentuated the wrinkles. I guess it doesn't really matter now. Amos doesn't mind if I have crow's feet.

I start rocking, Amos jumping onto my lap. I rock and rock, staring at 312 Bristol Lane. The car is gone, as it should be. It's Friday, I think. I wonder what she's up to over there.

I don't have to wonder long because pretty soon her front door is flying open. I think maybe she's coming for another visit. I could use a visit today. I could use something to cover up the feelings of loss from that trip down memory lane. But as she exits the front door, I know something isn't right. I actually push Amos down, standing, feeling solemn.

Something tells me I'm about to witness something that there will be no unseeing.

Chapter 16

The way she walks, the box in her arms hiding most of her frame, tells me she's angry. More than angry. Infuriated.

'Oh no,' I mutter to no one in particular, fear burning in my chest.

She's really off. Something's very wrong. I have no idea how to help her put the brakes on this out-of-control train.

She's roaring as she stomps down the front porch stairs. My heart patters. She's not even wearing a jacket, her bare arms out as she haphazardly flings the box into the front lawn before following it down and kicking it over with an angry foot. She boots the contents around the yard, flailing and kicking like a savage animal. She looks almost rabid, her face in such a contorted scowl, her screams and pounding fists on the box alarming me. She's kneeling in the snow now, garments flying all across the lawn. Red and blue shirts scatter in the snow. They're collared shirts. His shirts.

She's sobbing and screaming, and there's no stopping her.

It's time to get help.

I dash to my trusty phone. I'm ready to dial the emergency services. I hate to do it, but this can't go on. She needs help. Can't anyone else see it? Of course, who else is there to see this? He's gone, and it's just me on this street. I'm her only chance.

Before I get to the last '9', I see a car flying down the road, screeching into the driveway. How did he know? Did someone call him? Who could have called him? Maybe he had a suspicion when he left this morning that something was terribly wrong. Maybe they had another fight.

I click the phone, happy he's here. He'll help her.

Alex gets out of the car, initially just staring at his wife going crazy on the front lawn. She's still kicking his shirts around. He approaches her cautiously, hands out like he's approaching a deranged criminal.

She turns, and her scowl intensifies, if it's possible. She's shrieking now. The words are muffled, but I hear her screaming about 'late' and 'worthless' and other words that sound like invectives.

His hands are still raised, a surrender she's not accepting. His voice sounds calm, his muffled words half the volume of hers. He approaches her, talking gently.

She stands from the ground and punches him in the chest. He grabs her wrists. She keeps trying to punch at him, flailing like a crazed monster. She's whaling on him now, kicking, punching, even biting.

He needs to call the police.

I should call the police.

But I'm frozen, staring. I don't want to watch, but I need to.

The screaming and fighting continue. She breaks free, shouting in his face, pointing to the yard. Finally, her anger apparently bubbled over enough for one day, she stomps back up to the porch, whipping open the door and flying inside.

The door slams, and for a moment I think the glass might shatter from the sheer magnitude of the slam. It doesn't.

He's left in the driveway, pinching the bridge of his nose, nothing but cold snow and a mess surrounding him.

I want to go over, but what good will I do? What can I possibly do?

I stare, touching the window, my heart aching for him. He's a good man. He doesn't deserve this. Why is she doing this?

She's good. Deep down, she's good. But she's not good to him now. She's ruining everything.

After a few breaths, he looks around the front lawn. I wonder if he thinks about taking the box, shoving his clothes inside, putting them in the car, and leaving. I wonder why he doesn't just go. Yet I also understand why he doesn't. It's love.

She may not deserve it right now in many ways. He might be crazy for sticking around. But he loves her. And, who knows, maybe he feels like he needs her. Maybe he feels like he should be able to help her, to handle her. He's a man. She's a woman. What damage could she possibly do?

I feel like I'm there with him as he picks up every sad, abandoned, crumpled article of clothing from the frosty snow. I wonder if he picks them up so no one notices, to cover up for her crime, or if it's because he likes the numbing quality of the snow. Maybe he needs to feel like he can put something back in order, find some semblance of structure.

Where is that couple who kissed on the front porch? Where is that woman who chatted animatedly with him and danced in the leaves and loved him? Where is the woman I thought I knew, that he thought he knew? What's happened to her? And what will he do?

'Hang in there,' I whisper to the window, a pointless gesture,

I know. But it makes me feel better. I want to send him love, send him hope. I want to tell him that even from here, I know he doesn't deserve this.

Part of me wants him to leave. She can't appreciate him. She won't appreciate him if he sticks around. She needs help, major help. It's utterly, depressingly clear now. He can't give it to her. He just can't. He's too close to her to be objective, to know what she needs.

But dutifully, he finishes packing the box up, putting his clothes inside. He trudges up the steps, the box in his arms, and stops on the porch, a long beat passing. I think he's going to turn around and leave after all. He turns, looking at the street, looking at the car, and looking at the sky. Then, like he has so many other times, he just walks right in, shutting the door behind him.

After a moment, he wanders into the dining room, the box still in his arms. He drops it on the table before sitting down, his head resting on his arms on the table.

He sits like that for so long, I think he's fallen asleep. And in many ways, he has.

I'm about to peel my eyes away, to head off to busy my mind, when Jane saunters into the room, a strut in her step, a mischievous grin on her face. She walks like a woman with soaring pride, and my heart aches with the thought of what she's about to do.

She simply stands over him though, staring down at him, before looking up, out the window. My body constricts, my nerves ragged, as those wild eyes look towards me.

I shake my head in disbelief. Can she see me? Does she know I'm here? Is she looking at me, specifically?

The familiar questions lurch back, and I shudder. Before I

can stand, though, or reassure myself I'm just imagining things, she's gone, turned around with a quick spin and trudged into the blackness of the house I can't see.

He remains at the table, a lone figure in a dark, dark place.

Chapter 17

The days pass in an ambling string of moments, most of them spent mercifully in hours of sleep or in tense hours at the window. Some would say I'm obsessed, but what choice do I have? Sometimes, sitting at the window, I find my hands shaking as I study them, waiting to see what will unfold next.

It's not a joyful watching I'm a part of anymore. No, it's darker, more anxiety-ridden. It's a fear-filled watching I now partake in. Still, it is all I have. It's not like I have opportunity breaking down my door, places to be and things to see. Perhaps this is what hurts the most. I never realised that the emptiness of not having a family would carry over, would be most noticeable at this stage of life. I guess it's one of the unspoken fears of the childless. Who will be there when you need them most? There are no young bodies to painstakingly take on the weight of my reality. There are no grandbabies to hold, no chubby cheeks of grandchildren to brighten this solitary existence. There are no family dinners to ease the loneliness on holidays or birthdays, no photographs to take. There's just me and Amos and this window. The careful watching of the unwinding marriage across the street, of the dilapidated, sinister home that once was so joyful.

I'm biding my time, in reality. I am waiting for the next

plane out of here, to whatever is on the other side. I just hope it's a little louder, a little more vibrant, wherever I'm going. When did life become so darn quiet?

*   *   *

It's a week or so after the whole front lawn incident – time passes in such odd strings. I really never know what day it is. I think it's Saturday, though. It feels like Saturday. It was always my favourite day, the quiet fun of it. And his car's still in the driveway. He would be late for work if it wasn't Saturday.

He hasn't left her. It's something I've marvelled at all week. It's stirred a sense of respect in me, if not uncertainty. I don't understand how he can stay – yet I do. I get the loyalty, the idea that marriage, well, it's a commitment. Through good times and bad, that's what the vows say. He takes them seriously. Studying him as I have, I see that. He is a man who keeps his promises, even when she doesn't. Every day, at 5.01 p.m., he returns to what's becoming a house of horrors. It feels like a dark cloud rests above 312 Bristol Lane, mocking him and adding to the melancholy. Regardless, he comes home every night, loyal and dependable, too much so for his own good.

I sip my tea, rocking a bit as flurries gently cascade down. As if I've summoned him, he emerges from the front door. He's growing a beard now. I don't know if I like him with a beard. Maybe he doesn't, either. Who can tell?

He saunters out, alone. Always alone. She barely comes out anymore. It's not healthy. Okay, I know, I'm a hypocrite. But there's a difference. I'm cooped up by circumstance and age. She's cooped up by choice. That's not right.

He trudges through the snow to the car, pulls out and is gone. The tyre tracks in the driveway look eerie, a reminder that something's missing.

I rock back and forth, thinking a lot about the past, about years ago, about years before him.

I think back to one of my childhood memories; perhaps the snowflakes outside have reminded me of the snowflakes of that day. It feels like a different lifetime, like so many of the moments do these days.

* * *

For once, she wasn't nagging me. Maybe that's why it was such a good moment.

'You coming, Mother?' I asked, turning around as my sister ran up ahead. I was huffing and puffing, pulling my sled behind.

My sister was wearing a bright red coat. I always thought she looked stunning in the coat. In my own drab brown coat, I felt like I paled in comparison. My mother was beautiful, truly beautiful. She could've been a model or a superstar if she'd have put her mind to it. She and my sister looked like they were cut from the same cloth, truly. I didn't look like I was even made of the same thread.

Mom could have done so many things with those looks, everyone told her. Instead, though, she'd set her mind on my father, had us two girls, and had given up on any dreams of being someone else. I felt kind of sorry for her for that, but I understood.

Life didn't always work out, I grasped, even at ten.

'Right behind you,' she announced, her voice elegant, her red lips emitting the words with a grace I didn't know, didn't think

I'd ever know. Even trudging up a snow-covered hill, she looked sophisticated.

I clunked along, following behind my always-perfect sister, who was, of course, the first to the top.

She was always first.

Still, I shook off the cold thoughts as I shook off the cold, wet snow gathering on my shoulders. I readjusted my hat as I lined up beside my sister, Mom lining up beside me. The three of us stood for a moment, taking in the sight of the snow-laden hill. It was the best sled-riding spot, and it was all ours.

I looked at the perfectly covered hill, the snow untouched. For a long moment, I said nothing, thinking about how sad it was to ruin this unblemished spot. What gave us the right to mar it with our childish antics? Why did we feel the need to fly down the hill and disrupt this beauty?

But no one else was thinking about this apparently. Because before I could turn back, my sister was flying down the hill, screaming and laughing. My mother followed suit, the two of them racing to the bottom.

I stood back, looking at my feet in the piles of snow, my toes wiggling as I tried to see if I could still feel them.

From the bottom of the hill, they were giggling and laughing, waving at me to hurry up. They were always looking at me from afar. I was always in the distance, separated from them, their cacophony of laughs, of beauty and of joy.

'Now or never,' I whispered to myself, knowing I had to try. I couldn't stay behind. I had to try to emulate their joy. The exquisiteness of the scene was already ruined. So I sat down and sailed down the hill.

And as I flew towards them, the sadness of spoiling the scene, *the thoughts of being apart faded as I heard laughter swell. My own laughter, something I hadn't heard for a while.*

I'm back, *I thought.* I'm still here. That smiling, bubbly girl is still in here. I just need to reach out to her from time to time.

At the bottom, I skidded to a stop. I looked up, ready to finally be a part of the laughing, crying mess of females. For a moment, we could just be three females in the same family, out on a freezing cold day, warmed by our shared love and joy. For once, my melancholic tendencies wouldn't get in the way.

I turned to my mom and my sister, ready to share in the craziness of my slide, for them to comment on how great it had been. But, as I looked at them, I realised they hadn't noticed me. They were still laughing with each other, talking now about some new clothing store and how they needed better mittens.

I sat for a long time, waiting for them to acknowledge me. Tears stung in my eyes. It had been for nothing. That joyous ride, that brave step – no one had even noticed.

I fiddled with some snow on the front of my sled when my mother finally turned.

'Oh, are you finished? Did you go already?' she asked. I was an afterthought even now.

I looked up at her, into the eyes of the woman who shared my DNA but who wanted to share nothing else with me.

'Lucy, you want to go again?' she asked my sister, turning to her in the bright red coat.

'Race you, Mom,' she bellowed, and the two stood quickly, giggling and chasing as I sat, alone, at the bottom of the hill, staring at the now blemished hillside, the beauty gone completely.

I glanced up at them, the picture-perfect family, the girl I could never be. I knew for sure in that moment I would always be the girl my mother would never, ever truly love.

And once more, life was complicated and grotesquely lonely. I wondered if it would be like that forever, literally forever.

*   *   *

Apparently I've been in my memory for a long, long time because, before I know it, the mailbox is clinking with the presence of letters. I walk fast – well, as fast as I can these days – hoping I can catch Mr Anderson, the postman who started last year. He's young, two small children at home. He walks purposefully, the stride of a man with two young children, so he's gone by the time I open the door. It's a shame. He's good-looking and nice too. I could've used a minute to say hello.

I open the metal box on my house, pulling out junk mail, advertisements and a gas bill that will probably be way too high.

I almost shut the door, the cold air chilling me even though I have a blanket wrapped around my shoulders. I stop, though, at the sight of Alex's car pulling into the driveway. On the top is a snow-covered evergreen, the ends of it hanging over the front of the car in a way that's both charming and ridiculous. I smile.

A Christmas tree. Of course. It's almost Christmas.

Again, the dates and days sort of blend together. I'd almost forgotten.

The sweet man is probably hoping it will cheer Jane. I'm hoping for that too.

He gets out of the car and eyes the task at hand. I wish I was younger. I wish I could help him.

He looks over at me, and I smile. We usually don't have any sort of contact, his work schedule hectic and my body frail. We tend to keep our distance, not really by mandate or choice, but just out of circumstance. He stays over there, I over here.

I shut the door and wander back inside, heading straight over to my chair. I'm excited to watch this all unfold. They could use something to reconnect them, and Christmas is the perfect holiday for that, isn't it? Perhaps the holiday will be what bridges the growing gap between them. This could be the gesture they needed to fix things. I'm also selfishly happy because it'll be a small part of the holiday I can enjoy from here. It's the first Christmas tree on Bristol Lane in ... Gosh, I have no idea. A long time. Maybe too long.

He struggles with that tree for a while before finally, wrapped in a blanket herself, Jane emerges.

The first thing I notice is that she's different again. This time, it's not a subtle difference or a change in her stance. It's her hair. It's gone. Those beautiful blonde locks have been chopped in what seems like a haphazard way. It's one of those new cuts that reminds me of a rogue weed eater on the loose. Don't get me wrong, she's still strikingly beautiful, her features accentuated by the cut. But I miss her long hair. It's like she's trying to make the outside change with the inside – and there's a lot less hair to go with how there's a lot less of her, too.

She stomps outside, staring at the car. I wait for the smile, for a hug and kiss I haven't seen in so long. Instead, she shakes her head, says something to him in the angry stance and then turns on her heel. He hangs his head.

Can he do anything right? Doesn't she see that he is so good to her?

I feel so bad for him. My heart aches for him. Why is she being like this? Has she lost her mind? She'd have to have lost her mind to not see what he's doing for her.

I watch him slowly struggle with the tree, all by himself. I wish I had someone to go help him. But it's just me and Amos. We wouldn't be much help.

After a long while, he loosens the tree from its restraints, plopping it onto the ground and dragging it behind him into the house. Pine needles fall out, leaving a green path through the snow. Somehow, it's beautiful.

Eventually, I see him wrangling the uncooperative tree in front of the window, putting it into the correct place. I'm a little sad it's going there. It's going to take away some of my viewing ability. But, on the other hand, it'll be nice to have a tree to bring some holiday spirit. I don't have the energy to go in the attic and dig out all of the holiday decorations, and besides, I was never big on the holiday, anyway.

I've got one box of candles that go in the window. They are from the days when he was still around. He said they'd add some elegance to our simple home. Back then, I just found them to be a hassle, not worth the time. He bought them, though, and dealt with them. I broke one. There are two left, two that I've guarded with everything I have. No matter how tired I am, I always get them out now at Christmastime – when I remember it's Christmastime, that is.

This year, they're here across the street to remind me. I'll need to muscle up the energy to dig the candles out. Christmas is returning to our little lane thanks to them. How lovely it will be to have a decorated tree in view. I get a little misty-eyed, thinking of the lights and ornaments and how pretty the star will be on top – or maybe they'll put an angel? I do hope for an angel. Growing up, in the days before, we had an angel for the top of our tree. I get nostalgic thinking of those early years, the good times.

Things are different now, though. It's someone else's turn to celebrate, to make memories. I'm happy to get to witness them. I'll watch them decorate the evergreen and gather around it. I'll watch them stack presents and open them on Christmas. This will be lovely. This will help Jane see what she has.

She wanders into view now, her arms crossed over her chest, the blanket still cocooning her. An exchange occurs. She's yelling again. And this time she points her finger along with the yelling, her arm outstretched from underneath the plaid blanket.

Eventually, she shakes her head and extends an arm to hold the top of the tree. He disappears. He must be securing it.

She peers out the window now, looking at me. I think about waving, but that would be too much. I rock silently, just staring, watching as the tree jiggles under her grasp.

We lock eyes, and there's a slight smile on her face, but it's one that's unsettling somehow. I don't understand it, but it sends a shiver right through me.

The tree still jiggles as she continues to stare. Finally, after a long moment, she mouths something at me. She has to be looking right at me.

I squint, studying her lips, wondering what she could possibly be saying.

I make out the words, confusion swirling in me.

'Is this what you want?' she mouths, three times, perhaps in case I didn't figure it out.

Is this what you want? What does she mean? I don't understand. Is she taunting me? Why is she saying that to me?

She turns away now, her attention back on the tree, and it's like I've imagined it. But I know I haven't.

What is she talking about? It's such an odd thing to say. I feel like I could heave, the bubbling in my stomach mixed with a dropping sensation frightening me.

After a while, the tree is finally in place. He stands back up, reaching for her hand. She obliges. That must be a good sign.

I shove aside the odd statement. I must've misunderstood her. Certainly, she didn't mean anything by it. I shake it off, staring at them, studying the scene instead of analysing the words I thought I saw.

He pulls her in, and she lets him. For a moment, they're back to normal, standing beside their barren tree, just a normal couple waiting for the holidays.

I smile.

It's okay you don't have children, I want to tell her. *You can still make life beautiful. You have each other. That can be enough, really. If you take the time to appreciate it. And it's okay things haven't been perfect. It's not too late, not yet. You can turn this all around.*

I take a deep breath, hoping against all odds she'll listen to my silent, whispered words, that somehow the universe will help her hear them. I hope she'll heed my warning, take my advice. It's truly the only redemption of ageing – the hope that your wisdom, your mistakes, your regrets, can help someone else, that it all has a purpose.

Because if regrets can't at least change someone else's fate, then what's the point of it all anyway?

It's a hard thought to muscle through, the idea that maybe everything happened in vain, that all that suffering was just for suffering's sake, and that nothing I do can change anything.

Staring at them as snowflakes fall, though, I feel a twinge of hope. I hang on to it tightly as I stroke Amos, rocking in my chair and feeling, at least for the moment, all is well.

Chapter 18

Blanket wrapped around my shoulders, my blonde hair falling down my back, I rocked in the chair as I studied the falling snow. My shallow breaths felt like they were stabbing my lungs, tears welling in my eyes as darkness drifted over the lane.

Where the hell was he? Where was his car?

I rocked back and forth, squeezing the blanket tighter, biting my lip as I stared at the street like the fool that I felt like. What an idiot I was, sitting there like the abandoned damsel, at his mercy.

I hated myself for it. I hated the weakness in him that was rubbing off on me. Most of all, I hated him.

The rage had been building lately, and nothing he could say would make it go away. He could defend himself all he wanted, swear up and down that it was madness to accuse him, but I wouldn't be made a fool. I knew what he was doing, or more accurately, who.

And I hated being made to look like an idiot. I hated, more than that, how I'd let myself be in a position to need him. Hadn't I learned my lesson growing up? It was foolish to need anyone. You needed to rely only on yourself. I'd broken that golden rule, thinking love would change everything.

But it hadn't. It hadn't changed a thing. There I was, a damn housewife at his beck and call, childless, and not living the life I'd hoped for.

And there he was, some desk job worker without a prayer for promotion, without a spine, and without the ability to give me what I really wanted: a child.

We'd been through the protocol, the encouragements, and the doctors' visits. We'd been told to make peace.

But making peace had never really been how I did things. I arguably had different coping methods.

Sometimes, in the midst of our fights, a twang of guilt would creep in, a subtle pinging of my moral compass that what I was doing was wrong. But I couldn't stop it. The only thing stronger than my will to maintain power was my desire to make him hurt.

Plain and simple. He needed to be hurt. He deserved it.

A few minutes later, the anger now pure fury bubbling inside, his car glided down the street. I sat at the window a moment longer, waiting for the familiar sound of the car door slamming. I rocked, back and forth, back and forth, the momentum inciting my resolve.

The idiot I was married to was going to pay. The bastard would pay.

I heard his footsteps creep along the floor, his briefcase plop onto the table. I kept rocking.

'Honey?' he asked, the fool, using the term I'd come to hate.

'Where were you?' I spewed out, studying his reflection in the window. I smirked at the frailness in his stance, at how broken and weak he truly looked.

'We've been through this,' he practically whispered. 'The boss gave me another set of reports I have to do on Wednesdays. I'm only a few minutes later than usual.'

'You're right. We have *been* through this. Do you really think I believe that? Do you really think I'm a goddamn fool? I know what you're doing. Don't think you're going to get away with this – making a mockery of me. What, you think you can leave me? Do you?'

'You know I love you. I wouldn't do that to you,' he reassured me, still standing in the same position, his face pleading with me through his reflection in the window.

I tossed the blanket back, standing from the chair, turning to face him.

'No, you won't do that. You won't,' I commanded, calm and collected. He looked disturbed. He looked afraid.

I liked that I could still stir that *fear in him*. The feeling sent a chill through my body.

'You know this has to stop. You need to stop this,' he begged.

'Do I now?' I asked, leaning back on the windowsill. I took a deep breath.

'This isn't you. You know that, right? It isn't you.'

Those were the words that he shouldn't have said. Those were the words that were too much.

I stepped away from the chair, walking towards him.

'I really wish you hadn't said that,' I whispered when I was right in front of him.

And the genuine fear in his eyes only stirred me more.

Chapter 19

She doesn't knock. She comes right through the door.

Not that I mind. Despite all that's happened, we're still on an 'enter instead of knock basis', and I'm okay with that.

Since the Christmas tree, they've had a few quiet moments, a few interactions that have made me think maybe things will be okay. I've seen them on more than one occasion studying the tree or kissing goodbye on the porch. I've told myself the Christmas magic was working.

But then again, there have also been moments that tell me it isn't as picturesque as I'd like to believe. There have been shouting matches at his car when he comes home. There have been screaming fights so violently loud, I can hear muffled yells even from my rocking chair. There was something thrown at the window just last night.

Things are still unravelling, and even though she's visited a few times since the tree went up, her smile doesn't quite fool me. Things still aren't right. Then again, maybe they never were.

Amos meows, plodding over to her as she comes into the kitchen. I stand from the table to greet her, my sad piece of toast sitting on a lonely plate the centrepiece. The chill of the winter wind seems to follow her even though the door is shut.

She unwraps her scarf, brushes off the snow from her shoulders and drapes her coat on the chair. 'Hi, how are you?' she asks, her voice bubbly.

I smile. It's good to hear her voice, the one I recognise from before. I study her, the dark purple dress she's wearing contrasting beautifully with her hair. Even though her hair is short now, so short, it's still striking. The choppy look only accentuates her features even more. I see up close that she's beautiful, stunningly beautiful, long curls or not.

'I'm good. How are you?' I sit at the table, and she goes to put tea on, as is our custom.

'Great. I'm great. The holidays are coming up, and everything is perfect, you know?'

'Uh-huh.' I bite my lip, watching her frantic movements, listening to her hum to herself as she dances around the kitchen grabbing teacups. She's too … happy. Too calm.

But I know now it's an act. And that's what frightens me.

She continues on, her disillusioned cheer carrying her through the conversation as she sets a kettle on the stove. 'Doesn't the tree look lovelier and lovelier? We keep going shopping and buying more decorations. I just can't seem to stop myself from sprucing it up. But anyway, have you seen the stories lately? That Jessica, I'm telling you, she's headed for trouble with Clint. Can you believe—'

I put up a hand, walking towards her. 'Stop. Just stop for a second.' My words surprise me, and after I've said them, I take a breath. I really hadn't planned on saying anything. I really did just want to enjoy some tea, but it was unstoppable, I suppose. Sometimes you have to say something.

She shakes her head, as if she isn't sure she's heard me correctly. 'What?' she asks.

I take a breath. 'We need to talk.'

'Oh dear, are you busy? Because if you're busy, I can go.'

'Shh,' I say. 'Come have a seat.'

I usher her towards the table, feeling in control of the situation. Feeling like I need to take the lead here.

'Honey, listen. I'm worried.' I say the words slowly, as if I'm savouring each one as it exits my lips.

She stares, blinking for a long moment.

'About what? Is everything okay?' she asks. She smiles that sweet smile, the one that would usually make me smile right back. But things have changed, no matter how badly I don't want to see it. She's different. They're different.

And, as a consequence, this is different.

I feel an anger surging within me, beneath the surface. How can she sit here talking about soap operas and tea? How can she pretend everything is okay? How can she act like the Christmas tree is going to make it all better, make all the horrid actions disappear? How can they just sweep it all under the rug?

'I've been watching and I'm worried about you.'

'That's absurd,' she says, spitting the words towards me. She's claimed her defensive position, her body tightening, her lips in a pursed line.

'I've seen that things aren't okay. You're different, and I'm worried. I also see glimmers of who you were, of that loving girl. It's not too late, but you need to take a step back. All the yelling and fighting, it's not good for anyone. All the shoving and physicality. It's not right and you know it.' My words gain volume and seriousness as I continue, courage building. Someone needs to say it, and I guess it's got to be me.

153

'How dare you make assumptions. Who do you think you are – telling me what to do? You're just an old, lonely woman. You don't understand what it's like.' Vengeance seethes in her eyes, her posture tightening now. She sits taller, as if she needs to make her presence known. I notice her hands shake as one finds its way to her neck, grasping it and rubbing it as if she's easing the tension.

I continue, staring right into the face of the wolf across from me. 'But I'm telling you I do. I might be old now, but I wasn't always. And I know that this path you're heading down, it's ugly. It's going to leave you cold and alone. You need to get it together and bring it down a few notches.'

'Stay out of my marriage.' Her words are sharp, pointed and full of an energy that unsettles me.

'Stop abusing him,' I shout back, a strength in my voice I haven't sensed for a while making itself known.

She's taken aback, I can tell. I venture that I may have scared her a little.

She stands, stomping towards me, her face inches from mine, circling the table like a rogue shark. She leans in closer and closer until I wonder when she'll stop. An icy terror clutches my heart, but I fight to overcome it. I need to stand strong in this.

'Stay out of it. You don't know shit about me, and I won't have you trying to meddle with things. What, you think you're going to save the world from your rocking chair? You don't know anything. You can't do anything. So it'd be best if you just lived your life and forgot about ours. It's our business. Mind your own.'

She grabs her coat from the chair and stomps out, the door slamming. I shudder in the wake of the storm.

The kettle screams, and I jump, my nerves grated.

You know what's worse than witnessing someone falling apart? Knowing you really, truly are powerless. Knowing you really, truly can't do anything to stop it.

The kettle screams on for a long while before I remove it from the stove to quiet it. It's the next day, though, that screams of a human variety will change everything.

Chapter 20

The slow-progressing spiral downward begins with a confused, arguably idiotic, robin. Amos had been watching him for a few hours – and me, too, incidentally – out the window as we rocked on the chair. The cheerful bird flits and hops about, probably looking for bits of nourishment in the icy world outside. I feel a little sorry for him, thinking about how hungry he must be. Still, it's not my fault he got a bad lot in life – being a bird and all.

We sit staring. The candle is in the windowsill now – I'd dug it out yesterday, only able to find one. I was sad about that for a long while. Still, there's the tree across the yard in their dining room. It sort of feels like it could be mine, the sight of it cheering me. There's enough holiday spirit in the window of 312 Bristol Lane that from the outside, it looks like the perfect Christmas scene. No one would guess what's happened in the last few days judging from the beautiful display.

No one except me.

It's a bit sad when I think about it that despite all of the terrible things happening over there, they can still manage to outdo me when it comes to holiday décor. My lacklustre display is an exceedingly depressing reminder that Christmas no longer means much around here. I suppose it doesn't do to dwell on such topics, though. Besides, Christmas was never truly my favourite day.

In fact, for a long time, it was my least favourite day of the year.

But I digress.

Amos lets out sad little excuses for meows, which make me smile as we stare at the bird, harmlessly hopping about. And then, next thing I know, there is a smack against the window. The dumb bird has flown right into the sparkling glass. We observe his descent as his body slides down the window.

A horror expresses itself as a shriek, but inside, I am ... I don't know exactly. Surprised? Anxious? A little bit entranced?

Regardless, I just know nothing this exciting has happened in a while. Nothing that made my heart jolt in a way that I knew I was alive.

Amos jumps up from my lap in an excited frenzy, trying to leap at the window in a desperate act to get in on the excitement.

I find myself magnetised to the bird, walking towards the front door. I grab my coat from the hook, wrapping it around my shoulders as I carefully step outside into the freezing weather. The wind whips harshly, the porch offering a bit of protection. I tiptoe down the steps, not really sure why. I'm drawn towards the bird that lies in the snow now. I make my way around the house, to the window that's become my refuge, and I stand between my window and 312 Bristol Lane's dining room, glancing over at the house.

I return my attention to the reason I'm out here: the dying

bird. I think I see its wing flutter just a few times, the bird twitching with its oncoming death.

I stare blankly, feeling – what?

I thought I'd feel pity, watching an innocent creature breathing its last. I thought I'd feel compassion or empathy, or even frustration at not being able to help it.

But staring, I realise I'm simply dazed, studying it like some medical experiment, wondering how long until its breathing will stop, wondering if it understands what's happening to it. I wonder if it is curious about where it is going next and if it's any better than here. Do birds worry about things like eternal damnation and repentance?

What a ridiculous thought to have. I'm losing it.

Studying the bird as its life flickers out, I want to feel anything, something. I don't want to feel numb. But life has, in many ways, numbed me. Sometimes that is a blessing.

I stare across the yard at 312 Bristol Lane with a new perspective. Is this what she feels? Numb? Is she so cruel to him because she doesn't feel anything?

Or is it more monstrous? Does she, instead of feeling empty, feel pleasure from his sorrow, from the pain she inflicts? Is she moved by sadistic notions of hurt?

One can't tell, at least not from here, not from the window. But it is certainly something to consider.

When the wind becomes unbearable, slapping against my face, I turn to head back inside to my rocking chair. But before I enter the warmth of the house, I pause, glancing back at the now-dead bird.

There's no use in wasting a perfectly good bird, and there's no use in keeping Amos from what he truly wanted. I might as well make some good out of the creature's demise, make someone content. I know Amos will be happy with his death.

I stumble back the few feet to the bird, staring at the bloody carcase. I stoop down, my bones aching in the process, and scoop up the dead creature in my bare hand. The blood oozing from it is still warm and it feels sticky on my skin. I stare at the lifeless form in my hand, feeling how fragile it is.

I amble back up the steps and inside, holding the bird on my hand like my skin is a silver platter. I shut the door behind me. Amos is still sitting at the window, peering at the bloody snow.

'Amos, baby, I have a treat for you,' I say, walking to the kitchen to where Amos's bowl is sitting. Without another thought, I tilt my hand, plunking the dead bird into the cat's dish. 'You're eating real good today,' I add, wiping my hands together, the blood smearing on them. A few splatters have escaped from Amos's bowl, marring the floor around it. I ignore it. A little blood spatter isn't going to hurt anyone.

Amos dashes over to his bowl, his eyes widening at the sight as if I've just given him the key to the lost kingdom. He grabs the bird in his teeth and plods off to a day of tapping into his hunting frenzy that lies dormant due to circumstance.

I trudge to the sink, washing the blood off my hands, the water running red. I dry them on a paper towel before putting on the kettle for tea.

I stand for a long moment, thinking about the bird, about the house across the street. I eventually make myself a cup of tea, the ritual itself soothing, before heading over to my chair and claiming my view.

There's a mark on the glass where the bird hit, but I ignore it. I observe 312 Bristol Lane. Maybe it's just my imagination, but it is like a dark cloud has perched itself over the house. Sure, it's a gloomy enough day, the greyness of winter offsetting any brightness from the snow. But somehow, that house looks darker, more foreboding. It seems to scream at me in warning: *something's coming. Something's happening.*

And I don't know why, but sitting and staring at that place, a nervous tension builds within, a fear in the pit of my stomach not unlike the sickening anxiety of plummeting down a roller coaster or narrowly escaping being hit by a car.

It must be the fear, the terror that robin felt when it plunged to the ground for the last time – assuming animals can feel fear, can feel pain.

I rock slowly, methodically, my hands a bit twitchy as I sit in waiting, wondering what the day will bring, but feeling like it's going to be something mystically momentous.

* * *

I startle at the window, and Amos meows. I must've fallen asleep, but I'm awake now. I glance out the frosty pane, having to lean forward to swipe a spot clear. It's snowing, the flakes pelting down. But even through the dizzying sight, I recognise what's happening.

Even here, across the way, I can hear crashing, loud yelling and chaos.

I pet Amos as I watch the terrifying sight unfolding around their kitchen table.

She's frenzied, chasing him around the table like he's prey, and he's got his hands up like he's begging.

There's no stopping her, though. She's out of control again, but it feels different. It seems more intense this time, like an irrepressible explosion that simply can't be tamed. She cannot be controlled, and I wish I knew why. I think he probably wishes that, too.

The disturbing dance continues, round and round their table. She's gesticulating wildly, her voice harsh and grating even all the way over here. I stroke Amos, my breaths quickening as I watch the struggle, the fight. He throws a chair in her path to stop her, but she comes at him, taking a glass from the table and throwing it across the room. It smashes into the wall behind his head and he yelps.

I don't know what to do. I'm scared, so scared. I wish someone was here, someone who could help. I want to call the police, but I'm so entranced, so afraid to take my eyes off the scene. Scared that if I even blink, I'm going to miss something vital. As the only witness to this, I feel a need to pay attention, to not miss a beat. Still, how can I just sit here and watch it unfold? How can I let her do this? But then again, what can I do? What can I possibly do?

A single tear trickles down my cheek, warm and wet. It runs onto my lip and the saltiness is surprising. It's like my senses are heightened. The feeling of Amos between my trembling hands. The taste of the tear, the sound of the screaming.

It feels like I'm here but I'm not, like somehow I'm watching myself sitting here watching them.

The screaming and fighting continue for what seems to be forever. She's still feverishly waving, and he's still trying to calm her. And that's when things change. That's when the fiend emerges, the side of her I can never unsee.

Looking back on that day, I would say it was the point of

no return for the monster – no longer a woman – living at 312 Bristol Lane.

With that choice, she sealed not only her fate, but all of ours.

Chapter 21

I would have missed it if I wasn't watching so closely. If I had blinked, if I had turned away for a second, I would have missed the crucial piece of the puzzle.

For a moment, she pauses, and I think she's done. I think she's calmed down, that his safety is guaranteed. I naively think that we can all breathe and everything will just go back to normal.

But then I see it – her fingers creeping, creeping towards something on the table. It's beside the plate, and at first I think she might be grasping at the napkin to dry her tears. However, when she picks up her hand, there is a glimmer to the silver object in her hand.

A knife. She's picked up a knife.

His hands are up now, and he's backed against the dining room wall.

It's the dining room where they ate candlelit dinners once, where he asked her to dance. It's the dining room where they swayed in each other's arms what seems like a lifetime ago. It's where they should only have happy memories.

She's tainted that. She's ruined that forever. Maybe she's ruined everything with that single flick of the wrist, with the grasping of her fingers for the object that will never really be put down.

She walks towards him, the knife pointed directly at her target. I can't be sure, but from here, it seems like she's smiling, her lips curled up in a sinister expression.

He looks panicked, terror racking his body. He must know she's not bluffing, and he must know everything's changed.

She sashays closer and closer to him. His hands are up, his back against the wall. Trembling, his lips move, his eyes locked on her.

What must it feel like to be him? To watch the woman you love strutting towards you, wielding power and danger over you? What must it be like to be so afraid of the woman who sleeps beside you, who is supposed to be your life partner? What is it like to be terrorised in your own home, but trapped by a love you can't explain?

His lips keep moving, and I squint to make out the words. *Please.* He's saying please. He's begging the woman he loves, the woman he shares a life with, to show mercy. But at this point, I don't know if mercy is hers to give. I don't know if she's capable of anything but evil.

She puts her free hand on his chest and, if it weren't for the knife, it would be the most loving gesture she's shown him in weeks. However, the knife hangs in the air like a dart ready to pierce its target.

Please don't.

These are my words now. I'm murmuring them, chanting them. My blood is warm and tingly as I watch her, as tears fall. She needs to stop. This needs to stop.

I need to stop it.

There is a pregnant pause, a moment that seems to tick on

and on and on. I watch her as she presses against him, the knife taunting him and teasing him with what could happen. The fear in his eyes, in his posture, is discernible, even from here. My breathing is ragged, tears welling, as I consider the very real possibility that this is how it ends. I will bear witness the utter unravelling of them, of him, and of her. And the reality is there is absolutely nothing I can do about it.

Nothing at all.

My hands clench as I study the scene, the knife paused as if frozen, her arm unwavering in its intensity. His lips keep forming the words, over and over and over. *Please. Please. Please don't.*

But she doesn't waver, doesn't shake, doesn't seem to care.

She is resolute in her actions and righteous in her stance. She is unbreakable in her position of power. I hate her for that. With one jerk of the knife, she could change this narrative forever. My hands shake because I'm squeezing them so hard, my heart pounding out of the walls of my chest. In just one movement, 312 Bristol Lane could be transformed into a true horror story, even more terrifying than what it's been so far.

But before it all ends in a bloody mess on the floor and a final piercing of who they are, there's a flick of her wrist, and the knife falls to the floor. She wipes her hands as if she's got dirt on them, spins on her heel and saunters away. It looks like there's a bounce in her step, and her head's a little higher. She looks like she enjoyed it.

He, on the other hand, slides to the floor, out of sight. I wonder if he's crying. I wonder what's next. What could possibly be next?

I realise with a start that I've been barely breathing, my

lungs now gasping for air. I hear a wheezing and wonder if it's me. No, it's not me. My lungs are filled now. I've taken breath after soothing breath. My lungs are content.

But there's a clear gasping sound, a desperation echoing.

Confused, I glance down.

'Amos, oh dear, I'm so sorry,' I announce, freeing my hands from around his tiny neck.

The cat gasps, his tongue out as his lungs drink in the life-saving air. When he's finally recovered, I stroke him in apology. He jumps down, crouching suspiciously in the corner.

What have I done? Lost in the spectacle, I've almost strangled Amos, the only companion I have left.

I sit for a long time, thinking about the event I've witnessed and thinking about the feel of Amos's delicate neck between my fingers. His life was literally in my hands, and I almost let him go.

I almost let him go.

* * *

He's leaving her. I know it. He's going to leave her. What sane man would stay? No man is going to put up with this. Nobody puts up with this, right?

Sure, there are stories about this sort of thing. Gossip in the grocery store, murmurs in the pews. There are tense relations palpable from across the church, and there are harsh, jagged words that signify a sinister undertone to the happy pretences. I've had suspicions, just like everyone else. But this is different; 312 Bristol Lane is different from those grocery gossip sessions.

For one, he's a man. True, a bit of a passive man – but he's capable of standing up for himself, isn't he? He has the finances. He's not trapped like some of the women I've heard about in a similar position. He could get out. And, although he loves her, he's not possibly going to let her get away with this. He can't let her get away with this, he just can't. It's too dangerous for it to carry on.

It's the only thing that lets me sleep that night – knowing he's going to leave.

True, it's a scary prospect that she'll be alone, all alone in the house right beside me. It's not that I'm afraid for myself, not really. As I said before, I'm an old woman with little life left to live. Death doesn't scare me, so she can bring her worst. I can handle it. In truth, I'm afraid for her, of what will happen when she's left to her own devices.

I know I shouldn't care. She's shown her true colours, and I no longer believe with certainty that goodness will win. I think she may be too far gone now. Still, maybe it's an ode to the past or of who she was, but I can't give up on her completely. I care what happens to her, even if I shouldn't. I really believe there's something wrong, a sickness manifesting itself in her that she can't shake. It's her fault how she behaves – but I still feel badly for it. I hate watching her ruin her life. I hate that she's royally messed it up and there's no going back. And I don't want to bear witness to her further decline once he's gone.

But he's got to go. I know it, I'm sure he knows it, and she has to know it. What's her plan in all this? What, does she think he'll stay and be her puppet for the rest of his days? Does she really think there's no line? Does she really think she's not crossed it, time and again?

I don't feel like tea the next morning. I'm jittery enough as

169

it is. I need to see this play out, and my hands are already shaking like a drug addict's. Caffeine won't help. Maybe what I need is wine to soothe my nerves. It sounds perfect right about now.

I feed Amos, the cat still a bit rattled from yesterday. I speak to him in my most soothing voice, the most gentle voice I can muster under the circumstances. It's arguably a little bit shaky, but he sneaks over to his food bowl once the tuna hits the ceramic. There are still blood spatters from the robin in his dish. I wonder for a moment, did he devour it? And then I perch myself at the window like the dead robin, and I wait. I wait for the blood to spill, for the final shattering to happen.

Like clockwork, Alex leaves for work, his tie straight and his jacket on. He starts the car and peels out of the driveway. I'm pretty sure this is it. Even though he doesn't have a suitcase, I am confident he's gone, long gone. He's not coming back. Jane, just like me, is going to be alone.

I expect to see her wallowing today. I wonder if I'll see a glimpse of her pacing at the window, watching for him. I wonder if I'll get to see her chewing her nails and looking forlornly out the glass, feeling regret and sorrow for what she's done.

Does she realise what she's done?

She has to see that she's wrong.

And maybe it's the hope of seeing this, seeing some sign that she's not a total monster, that causes me to sit at the window all day, only rising twice to use the bathroom and once for a glass of water. I don't eat because I can't seem to muster up an appetite. I just need to see how this works out. I need to see how she sorts this out.

But there is no reward for my toil. She doesn't pace or

longingly look out the window. There are no tears or sad looks to hang hope on. She passes the window just twice, once carrying some type of food and once carrying a cup of coffee. The second time it looks like she's gone into the living room, probably to watch her soap operas.

In short, she acts like nothing has happened. Her movements, her whole demeanour is the calm, collected Jane I sometimes see. There is no sign of guilt or fear or of awareness of what she almost did yesterday. The woman wielding the knife yesterday is unrecognisable – the cheerful, ordinary version is back for the moment. I can't believe she isn't shaken by what she almost did, or more accurately, what she did. How can she just let it all go? How can she ignore the fact she stepped over a line yesterday? And does she even want to come back from it?

In short, I can't even fathom how can she go on after yesterday. I live across the yard, and my whole world's been turned upside down. I've collapsed in on myself, my thoughts a whirling mess of contradictions, fears and what-ifs. How can she just keep breathing, keep living like she didn't try to kill him?

But what surprises me the most, what really makes me crazy, comes later in the day.

Chapter 22

Alex comes home. He hasn't left.

But there's one catch – he's three hours late. That means he must've at least considered it. He must've thought about leaving. Maybe he even did leave, his car chasing dusty trails to unknown destinations. Perhaps he was long gone. Yet something changed his mind, because here he is, slowly pulling into the driveway.

I can't believe it. I'm stunned. What is he doing? What could he possibly be thinking? Why would he walk back into this?

Am I losing my mind? She did have a knife to his throat, didn't she? Did I imagine it? Because why else would he be back?

I pinch the bridge of my nose with my thumb and forefinger, taking deep breaths and counting to ten. My head is swirling and pounding, pain rippling through my body. I don't understand. How could anyone understand?

I open my eyes to see him, hands in his pockets, trudging up the driveway, up the stairs onto the porch. At the door, he hesitates, his hand on the doorknob. He turns and glances at the car and, for a moment, it seems like he's looking right at me. I think for a second he might wave or might come over. If he does, I'm telling him. I'm telling him what he needs to hear – get out. Get out before it's too late, before she does something truly maniacal, something unthinkable. Something more maniacal and unthinkable, that is.

But eventually his hand turns the knob, and he steps inside – to what, I can't be sure. You can never be sure.

I shake my head, squeezing my eyes shut. This is absurd. How could he do this? How could she?

Suddenly, I don't feel like living vicariously through 312 Bristol Lane. I don't feel hope or joy or company. I feel betrayed. I feel awestruck by how wrong I was about them, about what they could mean. I feel like I'm living a nightmare, the only witness to the dysfunction of the house across the street. And I also shudder thinking about what terrors are lurking ahead, Jane the ringmaster in this twisted sport.

I no longer like my prime seating or view. This window feels more like an execution viewing window, not a glimpse into a peaceful world I'm missing.

I rock gently, staring at the car in the driveway, sickened at what might happen next. But, like so many of us, I can't turn away. I can't stop looking. Human nature beckons me to stare on, to watch the disaster unfold, to see the tragedy. I've been called to be a witness in this covert trial unfolding. I just don't think I'm strong enough to do the job.

* * *

Time passes. How much time? I don't know when I come to how long I've been sleeping. I do know it's dark, the moonlight shimmering down onto 312 Bristol Lane, looking like some kind of Christmas card. This is no Christmas card, though. This is something very different.

I shudder, a chill from the frosty window wafting towards me. I pull the afghan from my lap up around my chin, tucking in for the sight across the way.

The moonlight casts an eerie glow on them, glinting off the silver of his car and the silver in her hand.

They're both outside. She's screaming, and a shoving match ensues again. This time, though, she's claimed a new victim. I watch him chase her, beg her to stop, as she sinks the knife into the soft flesh of the tyres, getting two before he tackles her to the ground, the snow around them as she cries and kicks like the beast she's become. The car sinks lower and lower, her damage done.

He sinks to the ground, too, and for a second, there's an odd peacefulness to the scene. It's like she relents, exhaustion kicking in. She collapses in to him as he almost cradles her in the snow, his arms locked on her wrists, the knife still in her grasp. She's sobbing, and he holds her. Down on the ground, the chilling white around them, I wonder if they can get back up. I pull the blanket even tighter around me, as if I'm the one sinking into the snow, as if I can feel it wrapping itself around me like it must be them.

The knife drops out of her hand, finally. She's given in, beaten at her own game. But she's still won. The car, deflated, isn't going anywhere for now, and neither is Alex.

Of course, it's not just a broken-down car that's holding him hostage. He's deflated, too, and I think even with four working tyres, he's not going anywhere. He's too far in. Like her, he's too far gone.

After a moment, he must loosen his grip, because she

stands in a perfunctory motion, swiping at her eyes, glancing at the car, and then, arms wrapped around her chest, she marches inside, leaving him sitting, staring, freezing.

She slams the door, and I watch him in the beams of the moonlight, wondering how a human being gets to that point. Wondering how a human being becomes willing prey, how someone becomes so chilled they don't even feel the knife stabbing in over and over again.

My hand finds my heart underneath the scratchy afghan. I feel the steady thumping of it in my chest, feel the blood pulsing through me.

I think about that for a long while after he's gone. I think about it as I stare at the spot where he sat in the snow, icy frost chilling him both externally and internally.

Chapter 23

Nine years old. A June day. No school.

I was out in the front yard, the sprinkler spraying wildly as my sister jumped higher and higher, screaming in delight in her orange swimsuit. Towel wrapped around my shoulders, I slinked off, hair drenched, letting the sun soak into my skin. It felt so good.

Still, I knew soon Dad was going to come out shrieking about all the water we were wasting. The fun wouldn't last. It never did.

I walked along the fence, a white fence with flaking paint. My nail scratched at one of the long, peeling strips, fascinated. I wondered how long of a strip I could get off. I picked at it with my fingernail as my sister, still laughing, dashed back and forth, back and forth.

I looked to the street, trying to avoid what I knew was coming – yelling father, crying sister, fun ruined.

It was pathetic-looking really, the mangy excuse for a dog. Its fur was dirty and matted. It shivered and shook, its tiny body violently quaking. It shook so much it could barely put one foot in front of the other on the empty street. It was pitiful.

Without thinking, I dashed out onto the road. The curly-haired dog stared at me, still shaking. I approached it gingerly.

'Hey,' I said, scooching down to the dog, noticing it didn't have a collar. I thought maybe I could save it. Suddenly, I felt lifted somehow. At nine, I'd found my summer's purpose. I was going to save the tiny dog.

It was good to feel needed.

In the middle of the street, the sound of my sister and the sprinkler still going on like an endless song on the radio, I reached my hand out, wanting to pet the dog, craving the instant connection with another being. I could already picture it, our days on the porch, our nights cuddled up in bed. But before I could seal the deal and stroke the cowering dog, a shooting, ripping pain shredded my hand. Its teeth sunk in. It was like a pain I'd never felt, a sawing, slashing pain. It burned.

It burned so much, I thought I was dying. I thought it was certainly what the end felt like.

The dog still attached, I shook my hand and kicked out of pain. My sister's shrieks of laughter were replaced with my screams of horror and agony. She rushed over, the dog having now let go of my hand. Blood dripped, and I studied the creature, still crouched down on the road, in shock.

I heard the screen door fling open; Dad's boots stomped on the faulty, rickety porch.

'What the hell?' he bellowed, and suddenly it wasn't my hurting hand that terrified me so much.

'Get out of here,' I screamed at the dog, who scampered off in the opposite distance. I wanted it gone, needed all evidence of it to disappear before he got to me.

I clutched my hand to my chest, warm, sticky blood slapping against my skin as I watched the creature scuttle off. Tears welled in my eyes, but I wiped them away, getting blood on my face.

Dad dashed over. 'What were you thinking? You can't just pet a goddamn random dog,' he gruffly announced, grabbing my shoulder to take a closer look at the damage to my hand.

My sister stood nearby in her swimsuit, her hair still soaking wet. The sprinkler was still running, I noted. He was going to be mad.

'I told her not to pet the doggy, Daddy. She didn't listen,' my sister sweetly offered, that sickeningly sugary smile I'd come to hate flashing up at my dad. Two years youngers. The baby of the family. The treasure of the family.

'You did not,' I argued.

My sister cried as my hand continued to pulse. Her tears were huge, cascading from her gorgeous blue eyes.

My dad pulled her in closer, in comfort.

'Daddy, it's so scary. Why did she do this? I'm scared now. I don't ever want to go outside again,' she whimpered through tears.

Her tears were fake; I could tell. She knew even then how to be an actress, how to manipulate, even at her age.

I grasped my hand to my chest, the blood still warm. I felt woozy now, standing on the street and watching everything flicker in and out.

'Look what you've done,' he announced, his words chillingly calm and quiet. He glared at me, his gaze stabbing into me as his chest heaved in anger. 'You moron. Look what you've done. Your sister's traumatised. Is that what you wanted? To scare her? To torture her? You're supposed to be the older sister, the smart one. But you're nothing but a worthless dumbass. Do you know how much we're going to have to pay for this? Do you know how much trouble you've caused? Get the hell in the truck.'

I shivered, both from the pain and from the terror of Dad's words.

'I'm sorry,' I whispered through tears. 'I'm sorry.'

'Get the hell in the truck, now,' he roared, his arm still wrapped around my sister as he led her into the house. I watched for a long moment as they walked around the water of the sprinkler. I glanced at the blood dripping onto the pavement, at the peeling white fence, at my mangled hand.

There was no one to put an arm around my shoulders, no one to dry my tears.

As my dad led my sister into the house to get his keys, she turned back to me, gave me that smug seven-year-old smile. She grinned so wide, the grin that said she always got the attention, always got what she wanted.

I inhaled wildly, the pain nothing against the feeling bubbling in my chest. I didn't know what it was, but I recognised it as an angry, churning sensation I'd felt before. And then, like an epiphany, the word came to me, blood smeared on my shirt as I stomped towards the truck: hate.

I hated her with everything that I was. And I knew that she had to be taught a lesson.

I just needed to wait for the right moment.

Chapter 24

A visitor. They have a visitor today, and I think this might change everything.

It started as a typical Saturday – I think it's Saturday because he didn't go to work today. The tyres were fixed days ago, and he's been going to work the last few days. So I think he would've gone to work if it was a weekday.

I'd pawed myself out of bed earlier, fluffing my hair after taking stock of it in the mirror, inwardly cursing the wiry mess I'm now stuck with. I've got that typical old-lady style, curly and not flattering. Of course, who is there to impress? The silliest things take hold of my mind these days, I swear.

I'd hobbled down the creaking steps, careful to avoid the third and fifth as is my custom. They've always squeaked, and I do hate that noise. It makes me think of the grating of a knife on a sharpening block. Always has.

I'd wandered down, greeting Amos, who is still a little wary of me. That cat really does hold a grudge, the damn rascal. I decided I'd show him. I gave him only half a can. You can't bite the hand that feeds you and all that.

Finally, after there was a tea in my hand and the blanket was wrapped snugly around my body, I'd settled into the chair, getting ready for the scene across the street. I'd wondered what it would be today.

Lately, there's no use wondering though. It's pretty much the same. Either the house is desolate, her tucked away doing who knows what out of sight, or there's a screaming meltdown between the two. I don't like the second scenario. I don't. But I can't tear myself away just the same.

In fact, I've been sitting at the window more and more lately. I haven't even made it out of this living room in days, maybe weeks. I haven't turned on the television or read any books. I had to drag myself to the market last week for supplies. I've even missed my favourite soap opera because I can't stand the thought of missing something real. I can't stand the thought of not witnessing something I need to see. And, in truth, I'm afraid. I'm afraid of what's going to happen. I'm afraid for him. I have this burning feeling in my chest that something, something terrible, is going to happen.

And that's when it happened. A new car, one I've never seen, screeched to a halt in their driveway.

In fact, thinking of it now, I don't recall them ever having any visitors. Strange for a couple their age. Then again, I don't think they're quite in the state to host a Ludo night or whatever game they're playing these days. I don't think any company of sane mind would stick around very long.

So when the car door opens, I'm stretching my neck so much that it hurts. The curiosity almost kills me as I wait to see who gets out.

An older lady with a greying hairstyle matching mine emerges from the driver's seat, her feet carefully finding their place on the driveway. She's wearing a blue hat and a long blue coat. She looks like the Queen of England or something, prim and proper in her attire.

Who is it? Is it Jane's mom? Alex's mom? A great-aunt? What is she doing here now?

I can't imagine Jane would've invited whoever this is over, not with everything happening. And why would Alex? Maybe it's an intervention.

Whatever it is, I shiver at the thought of what could go down.

The door slams, and at that, the front door opens. He materialises from the house, holding the door slightly ajar. He cranes his neck as if he, too, is curious.

'Mom?' I hear him ask, as if he doesn't recognise her.

So it's his mom.

'What are you doing here?' he continues, rushing down to greet her, letting the door slam shut behind him.

Her voice is dainty and mellow. I can't hear her. It doesn't echo like his deep, bellowing voice does. How disappointing.

I see her hug him in a gesture of what looks like maternal love and concern. Her hands gripping his shoulders, she pulls back, a serious tone and look on her face. I lean closer to the window as if seeing better will help me hear better.

I do wish that old woman would speak up. Doesn't she understand there are people here to think about, people who need the pieces of the puzzle?

Damn her quiet mouse-like voice.

She murmurs on and on, and I get the sense he's being lectured. He hangs his head like a sad schoolboy being punished.

She lifts his chin, looking at his face. Even from here, I can see the black eye.

He shakes his head. 'No, no, it's not like that,' he says clearly, almost yelling at her. He shrugs off her touch, clasping her wrists like he's done to Jane so many times. It's gentler though. There's a loving touch here.

I watch the look pass between them, a look of concern meeting assurance. I wonder what she must be feeling. Clearly, she's on to them. She knows more than she should, probably more than me.

I should be happy he has someone to care for him, but I'm not. A wave of jealousy creeps up. Who does she think she is, meandering in now? *I've* been here from the beginning, witnessing it all. I've watched the demise, been witness to the horrors. And what, she waltzes in now, the hero of the hour? She thinks she can just walk in and understand?

Or maybe I'm mad because I know she does understand more than I do. She knows the inside scoop, stuff I can't piece together from here.

I hate that. I hate her for that. An oddly possessive feeling stirs within.

So when Jane emerges, wrapped in that blanket, her face pinching into a look of disgust, I'm actually on her side. I'm not mad at her for once, despite the barking, discordant voice that follows. I actually feel okay when she clomps down the steps, getting in the Queen Elizabeth lookalike's face and shouting, threatening her.

For a moment, Alex's mom stands firm, even in the face of chaos that has rained down upon her from her daughter-in-law. Hands on her hips, I see her stand tall, as if she's not afraid. But I know she should be. I've seen what Jane is capable of. She shouldn't be so sure she can stand up to her. Sure enough, Jane's rage is only incited more by her mother-in-law's refusal to back down. She takes a step forward, a familiar fury in her eyes. Finally, his mom must realise what I already know: she's in danger. This woman is unchained, uncontrollable, and not someone to mess with. I see the moment this realisation strikes her. The Queen shrinks back to a mere peasant, her stance crumpling in on itself, her arms removed from her hips. She takes a step backward like a cowering dog frightened by a swift kick from its master.

A long moment of hesitation occurs as the two women study each other. Eventually, Alex puts a hand on his mom's shoulder, and an exchange ensues. Jane isn't pleased, but she doesn't move a muscle, perhaps afraid to be perceived as giving in. After a few moments, his mom slowly turns, giving a few pointed glares at her daughter-in-law. She opens the car door, reluctant to give in but perhaps feeling like she has no choice. The tension cuts through the scene, the three of them dancing a reckless dance in which someone or perhaps even all of them are at risk of being destroyed.

I smirk a little when the fallen Queen sinks into her car, Jane charging towards her. His mom slams her door, but this doesn't stop Jane in the least. She pounds her fists on the window as Alex pulls her back. The car speeds away from them, and for a moment I think maybe the older woman is going to run over Jane. My heart stops, fearful that this scene will play out very differently than anyone could have imagined.

She doesn't though. Instead, she speeds down the street, pausing a hundred or so metres down the road. I wonder if she's going to turn back. I wonder what it must feel like to be her, to be so ineffective at protecting your own child. For a moment, I actually feel ... something. I don't know what. I think about what it must be like to stand by and watch the demise of your son. I wonder how it must hurt to realise the black eye he is sporting isn't from some gallant effort at a bar or from some rebellious sting with the law.

I wonder what it's like to know the woman your son loves isn't good, stable, or sane, but also knowing you have no ability to stop it all.

I wonder what it must be like to feed into the lies, to tell yourself he can handle it when you know he can't.

Above all, I wonder what she'd have said if she could've rolled down that window one more time, could've said something to impact upon him. But she didn't, the woman standing between the two of them so out of control that no moment could pass.

For a moment, despite the jealousy and possessive feelings, I think I might feel sorry for the fallen Queen. I realise that like me sitting here in my quiet house, she is also powerless, which is never a good thing to be.

Never.

There is a sense of the dust settling once the car is out of view, and for a few moments, I think everything will be fine. The danger has passed. But I should know better than that. Danger is always close by these days, lurking in every facet of this lane. No one is safe.

It's as if she's striking a match or flicking a light switch, because within seconds, she turns and flails him. The solitary moment of calmness is usurped by the anger within her and her hunger for violence I've come to understand all too well.

Still, I can't help but think about how happy I am that his mom is gone. I'm not ashamed to admit that I am glad she left. *Mind your own business.* Like it or not, it's all on me. I've got to see this thing through, and I don't want any distractions. I don't want anyone else coming in and claiming victory, figuring it all out.

I'm possessive of 312 Bristol Lane, even if they're not the kind of people one would be proud to own. They're mine. I'll carry the burden myself.

Chapter 25

Idon't know why I still keep my appointment. It's probably just a product of boredom, in truth. What good can a doctor do at this point? It's like buying an engine for a car you don't have or going to the salon when you don't have any hair.

Still, I go religiously. Perhaps I'm less okay with death than I tell myself. Maybe, somewhere deep down, I feel like I have unfinished business. Or maybe I'm scared to face the harsh realities that probably await me in the next life. I don't think I'm as sure of my afterlife status as I would like to think. A forgiving God sounds nice ... but I don't know if I trust in that completely. Some things just can't be forgiven, you know?

Or my frantic clinging to life could be Jane and Alex's fault. Maybe they make me feel – needed. It's an odd feeling to have, all things considered. Nonetheless, I've learned you have to acknowledge your feelings and honour your emotions. Or maybe that's just what a therapist once told me. I don't know anymore. When you get to a certain age, it's almost impossible to tell what is your own original thought and what you've heard from someone else. But I guess it doesn't matter, anyway.

My trustworthy station wagon creeps between two lines in

the desolate car park. No one makes an appointment at this time of day. No one but me and the other elderly patients whose only excitement is a doctor's appointment. It's pretty sad, really.

I waddle through the car park, the drizzle falling on my hair, but I don't mind. It's not like the doctor's much to look at and, even if he were, it's not like I'm much of a canvas to take in, either.

Not that I'd want that anyway. Doctors were never my type. Give a man a degree and a coat, and he thinks he's God. I always hated that kind of attitude in men, even if at one point I envied it. Some men get power and it goes to their heads. Some men get power and they think a woman shouldn't challenge them for it. I've always found doctors to be dreadfully unbreakable.

When I gloriously reach the waiting room, I'm a little out of breath but no worse for wear. I march to the counter and tell the receptionist – who is quite the bimbo, looking at me and asking why I'm there – that my appointment is at seven.

'No, it's at eight,' she says, smiling through her perfect white teeth at me like this is an appropriate time to smile.

'Look again,' I reply. I know how to deal with people like this, people who think they know better than me. True, I forget things sometimes. But I'm not a damn fool. I won't have this woman insinuating I'm the idiot. The scrubs she wears have brightly coloured sunglasses all over them. Sunglasses. Who wears something that hideous? She must be an idiot.

'Well, the doctor has other patients to see, you know,' she sasses back.

'Well, maybe he should get a receptionist worth a dollar,

then. Honestly,' I reply, anger boiling. I tell myself to calm down, though. What's the hurry? I have nowhere to be. And it won't do to make her mad. Although it could be fun. But it's not about time or how much I have. It's about being accused of being wrong. It's about no one taking me seriously.

'Kids these days,' the woman across from me says once I've sunk down into the padded chairs. I try not to touch the sides. If I'm going down sometime soon, I'd rather it not be from some flesh-eating bacteria that's probably residing on the armchair. I've seen the type who come into this office.

'It's not just kids. It's people in general. How can they be so dumb? It's like the whole world is full of imbeciles,' I mutter, glancing at the woman in a pink raincoat.

It feels good to complain. I'm grumpy today.

Of course, I may be grumpy every day – I just don't realise it. Loneliness has a way of confusing your feelings. It's hard to feel one way or another when you're alone with a cat, photographs and a window all day.

I wait for a long time in the room that reeks of bleach and medicine. A little boy sits in the corner on his mom's lap, snot running down his face. He coughs. I take a tissue out of my purse to cover my mouth. I don't need the little brat's cold. I'm achy enough, miserable enough.

Staring out the huge windows, I tell myself to do a feelings assessment like the one the doctor told me about. When I get mad or enraged, I'm supposed to ask myself what the source of the anger is. In truth, I don't even know what it is. If I had to pinpoint it – well, I couldn't. I'm just angry. It happens, right? I'm too tired to assess anything right now. I just want to sit here and breathe. I think I've earned that.

After what feels like an eternity and exactly seven coughs

191

from the brat in the corner, a grouchy, heavy lady calls my name. I smirk a little to myself, thinking how ridiculous it is to have such an obese woman working as a nurse. Does anyone recognise the irony? Isn't this supposed to be a health centre? Someone should take their own advice. She leads me through the door in the waiting room, taking me to another room that smells of bleach but still feels equally as full of germs as the waiting area. She pulls me into a side room to take some basic measurements.

I roll my eyes as she makes me stand on the scales. Pretty sure stretchy pants fit over any weight gain. And pretty sure I'm not gaining much weight eating – well, I don't even remember what I've eaten in the past few days.

I'm led down the hall of diseases to a little room, where she plops me on scratchy cardboard-like paper that crinkles way too much. I hate the crinkle. I try to sit as still as possible so I don't have to hear the crinkle.

I sit in the room, alone, some elevator music that predates even my glory days blaring. I look at the walls, the hideous yellow walls. They must've been inspired by vomit when they painted in here. Honestly, I love yellow. But this yellow – no. It's a foul yellow, reminiscent of that weird story about the insane lady and the woman crawling out of it. What was that story? It must have been a lifetime ago I read it. I did like it, though, the melancholic tendencies of the lady telling the story. How she got back at John. I get goose bumps just thinking about it.

I sort of wish a lady would crawl out of the paper now. At least it would give me something to do other than analyse how cold it is, how crinkly the paper is and how ugly the room is.

The doctor finally strolls in, whistling like he's having a good old time. It's a new doctor, one I haven't seen. Or, at least, one I don't remember.

I hate him already. Whistling, here? No. Just no.

But he whistles on, some ridiculous tune. No matter he's an hour late for my appointment. No matter I'm freezing, miserable and achy sitting on this damn table. No matter the wall is hideous yellow. It doesn't bother him. Why would it? He just whistles jovially. He was probably making love to that fat cow of a nurse in the other room instead of coming in to see me.

I just want my arthritis medicine so I can leave. Maybe it'll help me not feel so grumpy. Maybe these aching bones will feel better. Maybe he can up my dose, give me some of those good painkillers I had once.

I smile. I need to play this up, play smart. Manipulation used to be my middle name. I think I might be rusty, though.

'So, how are you?' he asks. He sits on the stool across from me, staring up at me. His bald head is sweaty. I hate the sight of those droplets on it. Can't he feel them on his head? Why doesn't he wipe them? Is it so hard?

'My bones are aching. It's difficult to get around. I think I need higher dosages on my meds.'

He chuckles, like aching bones are hilarious. Men. Doctor men. I fight the urge to roll my eyes. Or to grab the bin of medical waste, dig out a dirty needle, and stab him in the groin with it. I told you I'm feeling grouchy.

'Well, dear, I don't know about that. Let's see your chart.'

Code for: he has no clue who I am or what the hell I'm on.

'Sure thing, doctor.' I offer him a sweet smile and coyly tilt

193

my head like a sad, ill child. I fold my hands as if in prayer and swing my feet. I let him pretend he's better than me, smarter than me. I let him feel in control. That's the key to these kinds of men. Let them think they're in charge.

'Well, looks like we could up your dosage a little bit. But if you have any side effects—'

'I'll come right back in so you can sort it all out,' I reply like the frail old woman he wants me to be.

'And as for painkillers, I'll prescribe you a few low doses, but nothing too extreme, okay? I don't want you getting hooked.'

'No, wouldn't do to get hooked.' I wink at him now, grinning.

'Now, looking at your chart, you're also taking lurasidone, right?'

I nod. 'Yes, doctor, of course. Never skip a day,' I reply, smiling like an imbecile who swallows the pills like a good little girl. Like I'm under the influence of the drugs they've tried shoving down my throat for decades – and for decades, I've played along.

It isn't hard. Who is there to tell on me? Who is there to check on me?

It's kind of funny actually, to dupe him. I mean, he's supposed to be the doctor – yet he has no clue. He has no clue that I'm able to keep it under control, that I can act like I'm on those idiotic pills when I'm not.

I'm not as sick as they want me to be. I'm fine actually. I know what's best for me, and I know those meds aren't it. But I can play along. I've learned in my life that sometimes you must simply play the game to get what you want or need.

He goes through routine checks and diagnoses me as healthy and fit. After feeling about his pocket for a while looking for the prescription pad but unsuccessful in locating it, he tells me he'll leave the prescription at the checkout.

When he leaves, I cackle a little to myself. The blank prescription pad's in my hand. He'll never suspect me – delicate, smiling me. He'll think he misplaced it. He'll think when he was having sex with that cow or getting a blow job from the receptionist that he dropped it. He'll unpack a new one, forget about it and I'll take this one home.

I don't use them. I never do. It's more about the thrill of pulling it off. I'm not some frail old woman. I'm still crafty. I'm still capable. It's when you lose your craftiness, your manipulation, that you lose control.

Not today, though. Definitely not today. *Today, I'm winning this whole damn thing,* I think as I tuck my wrinkled skin back into my clothes, the prescription pad in my waistband as I leave.

Another addition to my collection – and some arthritis meds to boot. Perfect. I really did need those. Of course, I didn't have to come here, not if I didn't want to. I've got a few stacks of these at home. Just a few forgeries, and the pills could've been mine. What was the point of the trip then?

I don't know. I guess I just wanted to prove to myself I can still win. Because at home, who is there to win against? I needed to prove I can outwile, can outsmart.

And I did it. No one suspects an old lady to be capable of much, just like no one suspects the innocent-looking lady next door to do what she does.

195

People are so easily hoodwinked into believing what they want to believe. People are so easy to fool, to deceive. But not me. I'm on the winning side. I'm always on the winning side, no matter who tries to stop me.

Chapter 26

His heavy snoring prevented me from falling asleep. I slunk out of bed and crept to the seat by the window, staring out into the darkness of the middle of the night. A crescent moon cast its beams onto the house next door in an eerie yet poetic way, but I couldn't help feeling something completely different than serenity.

I felt vehemence, a familiar emotion surging even though I'd tried so hard to suppress it.

As if subconsciously sensing all was not well, even while he was asleep, he rolled over in bed, readjusting. The snoring started up again, and I bit my lip to hold back the quivering. I glanced at his body, breathing so loudly to announce the fact he was still alive. I thought about how easy it would be to end it all, to put a stop to the snoring, and to be free from the contract I'd signed up for.

What was wrong with me? It had been a question swirling in my psyche for years and years. In the two years since we'd gotten married, I'd thought I could suppress the unsettling thoughts, the fits of anger, the unresolved sense of something being off. When I'd said 'I do' to a life with him, I thought I could be different. I thought all those things that had haunted me in my youth could stay in the past.

But more and more, I'd come to realise the person lurking within me was rising up. She wouldn't be suppressed forever.

I had everything I could've hoped for. I had a nice enough house, a man who loved me, and a life many women would kill for.

Yet, for me, it was a life I would kill to escape from. I hated the feeling of being trapped, of being at his mercy. I hated the reliance on him. Most of all, I hated his weakness, his inability to be a man. I hated the fear that if he wanted to, he could ruin me. He could make a choice and destroy what I had. With one decision, he could shatter my reputation, my pride, and my strength. I hated that he had that power.

I had a life so many would want, but it wasn't the life I wanted, I'd come to realise. Sure, a huge part of it was that we hadn't been able to conceive, and I knew without a doubt it was his fault. I couldn't help but blame him for it, no matter how irrational that seemed. It was his fault, plain and simple. He'd taken the one thing I'd thought I could find purpose in away from me. Despite the house and the simple life, I found it was lacking in so many ways. And even if I knew somewhere deep down it wasn't true, I couldn't shake the feeling it was his fault.

It was all his fault.

In the past months, I'd found myself growing edgy with a toxic energy I didn't know what to do with. Everything about him suddenly irked me. And not in the frustrated housewife who giggles about socks strewn about kind of way.

I was irked in a way I'd felt once before in my life, a powerful urge to put a stop to it all ringing in my bones. I was itching to act, to rise above, to show my power. I was dying for a chance to end the endless cycle I'd been trapped in.

I craved a chance to make a statement.

I clutched my head, a splitting pain piercing through me. I needed to stop. I couldn't do this. Rocking back and forth gently in rhythm with his snores, I told myself it was no good.

She had asked for it in so many ways. The retribution I'd delivered to her wasn't entirely uncalled for. But this was different. This would be a new level.

He didn't deserve it. I knew it. I recognised it. He was nothing but good.

Still, that didn't stop me from wanting to be nothing but evil. I recognised the feelings for what they were, a devilish urge I couldn't stop. Or perhaps I didn't want to stop it.

I knew, though, this would be a new line I couldn't cross.

Still, staring at the moon beaming down, the stars dotting the sky in a magnificent way, I knew without a doubt that I couldn't just sit by. I couldn't just be the perfect housewife. Things were headed down a dark path, and I couldn't stop them.

I didn't want to stop them.

I wanted him to suffer if for no other reason than for the fact I could make it happen. I liked the feeling of that, my fingers tingling with possibility. There was certainly a line, but I could tiptoe right up to it, make him pay for all of his weaknesses. I could make him understand that it's a tough world and only the hearty survive.

Feeling a calm sense of resolve, I snuck back into bed, pulling the covers up to my chin. I rolled over, looking at the man beside me, thinking about how the love I'd once thought I felt for him had blazed into another emotion, one with just as much fervour but of a different kind.

Chapter 27

She knocks at my door, and I spring up. My bones aren't aching today, the extra milligrams or whatever the doctor prescribed doing the trick.

The prescription pad was burning against my skin, begging me to use it. I thought about what kind of numbing drugs I could get, ones that could take away every ache. But I didn't. It wasn't that I was scared. I guess I just like the pain sometimes. It's an atonement for — well, for everything. The pain reminds me that I'm still alive and still breathing. It reminds me I'm not quite done. I've never really taken the easy way out — at least no one can accuse me of that.

More knocking, snapping me back to the present. I seem to be drifting away a lot lately. I need to be careful. It doesn't do one any good to visit the past so frequently. I need to stay focused.

The pounding on the door echoes rapid-fire through the hallway, the feeling of desperation kicking in. I pause, standing in limbo. I need to get to the front door, but I look back, the shut door in the kitchen almost calling me today. I've managed to ignore the door for the most part for the past few months. It's blended into the background, my psyche pushing every fleeting thought of it aside. Today, though, it seems to scream out, and it makes me uncomfortable that the door is making itself known today. Why today? I study the shiny brass knob that hasn't been touched in so long. It's like it's beckoning me to come over, to look at it. I shake my head, the knocking louder on the front door.

It wouldn't do to go to that other door. I need to go to the front door, the one I can open without fear.

But, as I saunter down the hallway, a sensation takes over me.

Terror.

It's almost numbing, the unfamiliar feeling creeping inside and grasping me. What am I afraid of?

I don't like the feeling. It makes me feel weak.

I shake off the icy anxiety, shoving it down. Still, as I trudge to the door, I realise an unsettling fact: she scares me a little bit. Actually, she terrifies me. I tell myself to be brave. I'm stronger. I'm wiser. I'm more wily than even she is.

I put my hand on the front doorknob, entranced by ... what? What is it about her that's so mesmerising? It's almost like she's the shut door in the kitchen, a brass doorknob I want so desperately to reach out and grasp but can't.

I think I've known for a while she's something mysterious, maybe since the first day. The petite frame that seemed to drip with sweetness and joviality. The endearing smile, the sinuous voice. Like a siren, she lured me in, just like she did him.

But now I see beyond the surface. I see the cracking, peeling skin. I see that behind the siren is a beast, luring those around her to their ultimate demise – a demise worse than death.

Still, I can't say no. I can't stop being drawn to her. I can't, even against all rational thought, believe she's a lost cause.

Before I turn the knob, Jane has opened the door, invited herself in. It feels – intrusive.

I don't say a word, letting my frigid gaze do the talking for me.

'Hi,' she says, bubbly. It's a far cry from the woman I witnessed just the other day or in the past weeks. Her entire being, her full aura, has changed again. It's like her personality is this fluid being, drifting back and forth in a cacophony of utter confusion. There's a constant pushing and pulling, an unsteadiness that only intensifies the dichotomy in her character. She's an enigma, and even though I'm determined to sort her out, I don't know if I ever will.

My gaze rests on the item in her hand. A bottle of wine.

'I thought I'd liven today up a bit – what do you think? I mean, I got my cleaning done last night, stayed up into the wee hours, because I have a plan. What do you say you and me forget about all this blah weather and the grey, rainy day? How about we just have some fun? What do you say? Could you use some fun?'

By her wild hand motions, I'm guessing the cracking open of this bottle won't be her first indulgence of the day. And what, is it even noon yet?

'I don't drink anymore,' I reply, but even as I say the words, the liquid tempts me. I can almost taste it, and though it's been years – has it really been years? – the craving resurfaces.

'Don't be ridiculous. One glass won't hurt you.' It's almost a demand, not a friendly invitation.

The temptation builds, my hands sweating a little. I should say no. But my body aches. My head hurts. And she's so … happy. I don't want to taint that, no matter how false the surface-level joy is.

'Just a half a glass,' I agree as she emits a little dance and squeal, heading to the kitchen. She riffles through my cupboard, searching beyond the familiar ceramic mugs for wine glasses.

'They're on the top shelf,' I say, thinking about how much dust must be on them, thinking about how long it's been since I've had an occasion for wine glasses.

Even when I hadn't sworn off the vice, I just drank from the bottle. It was easier that way. There was no drinking for appearance when I was drinking alone – it was imbibing purely for the numbness, and there were plenty of days, lonely nights, that those bottles numbed me to the perfect level.

I think maybe that's what she needs now, too. She needs to feel the sweet, cradling feeling of nothingness. I can't blame her completely.

'I'll just hop on a chair,' she says, skipping over and dragging the heavy oak chair like it's a feather. She jumps on it daintily, stretching for the glasses in the back of the cupboard as I take a seat.

After an eloquent dance of balancing glasses, dusting them off, and opening the wine – it takes a while to find my wine opener – a half-full glass of the devil's liquid sits in front of me. I hold it to my nose, wafting in the grapey smell with a hint of potent vinegar, closing my eyes.

Sometimes just a smell can take you back, and even though it takes me back to those times in my life when I, too, needed numbness, I can almost feel the warmth soothing my weary veins.

'Day drinking. So underrated, huh?' she asks, clinking my glass in cheers. Cheers to what? What is there to celebrate?

'Everything okay today?' I ask, knowing the answer already.

I set the wine glass down, fiddling with the stem in between my fingers. I'll just look at it for a while, savour the feel of the glass between my fingers. My fingertips dance up the slim, fragile spine of the glass, tracing the curvature at the base of the bulb.

'Is it ever?' she asks, rolling her eyes. 'Honestly, I don't know how much more I can take.'

The veil of alcohol lifts slightly, just enough for me to see her true face. The glimmer of the front-yard woman is lurking just beneath the surface. I'm much better at detecting the monster that hides there now that I've seen it rear its head in truth.

'Well, can I help?' I ask, staring at my glass of wine, watching as the liquid cascades in the glass as I carefully roll the stem back and forth in my fingers. She plays with her glass too, quiet for a moment, as if in thought. I lift the glass to my lips, savouring a final whiff before committing to the first sip, the liquid hitting my lips with a familiarity that soothes. I've missed it so much, I realise as I swallow the first sip, feeling it trickle down my throat. I close my eyes, relishing it before taking another swig.

Finally, she breaks the silence.

'Yeah, you can knock some sense into that husband of mine. He's not going to get away with it.'

I glance across the table now and see the quality in her eyes I recognise but also fear. I hear my heart pounding in my chest, the thudding mixed with the swirling wine – a concoction for disaster.

'Think you've already achieved that, haven't you?' I ask, testing the waters with my voice.

She stares back at me. 'Excuse me?'

The words are a stark contrast to the gentle quietude of the house. Every syllable exits her lips like a whispered prayer, but the bite of the first word gives away the edge in her voice, stabbing into the contented atmosphere between us.

'I've seen you with him. Don't you think maybe you should tone it down?' The words are hard to say but necessary. I know the risk of saying them. Things got so ugly last time. Still, I can't just pretend anymore. I can't let her get away with it. She needs to hear them, and I need to say them, no matter how this all turns out. I take a deep breath, wondering how the words will sit today and fearful of the worst. The wine must have dulled her senses, though, because the reaction this time is less vehement than last time.

'Try living with him and you'd understand. The pretentious prick acts like everything is about him. And I know what he's up to. He's not getting away with it. Did you know he was ten minutes late yesterday? Swore it was because of a traffic accident. Didn't hear the fire whistles. Didn't hear the cop cars, did you? He thinks I'm a moron. And his stupid mother coming over the other day to meddle. I can't believe I married a goddamn mama's boy. *Pathetic*.'

She raises the glass to her lips, chugging on the liquid, her eyes actually closing as she does.

'I think you're losing control,' I say, a bit more fear rising within that I don't want to acknowledge. Still, someone has to stand up for him when she won't. Someone has to point out the truth she's too blind to see – or too far gone to want to see.

'What, you're actually taking his side? I didn't peg you as so pitiful.' She snickers and shakes the wine in her glass in a cavalier move. She doesn't get it. She really doesn't get it.

'I'm taking both sides,' I retort, my voice edgier now. 'I'm trying to save both of you. Can't you see? You're on a dangerous path, and I don't think you're going to like where it ends up.' I'm standing now, towering over her. Even at my short stature and with my frail frame, I feel powerful standing above her. I like how it makes me feel. I haven't felt this power in a long time.

I walk around the table, her evil glare on me. I sink down beside her, eye level with the woman who isn't a stranger but isn't quite a friend either. Maybe I'm emboldened by the few sips of wine, or maybe by the morality of what I'm about to say. Maybe I feel, deep down, that this is my chance to make amends for my own mistakes.

Whatever it is, I feel brave when I inch closer, my breath slapping her in the face.

Coolly, rationally, I spew out the words I've been wanting to say. 'You need to back off. You're losing it.'

She doesn't move back even though I'm invading her personal space. She locks eyes with me, maintaining the uncomfortable, tense position. I can feel each exhalation from her nose on my face. '*You* need to back off. I think *you're* losing it. I don't know what you think you know, but I know what's best for me. I'm not going to let him ruin my life. You have no idea what it's like. So don't you sit here judging me.'

I glower at the woman who has enchanted me and also horrified me. I gape at the woman who will be the ruination of herself, of her husband, maybe of me. I stare at all the dreams I had of watching a beautiful love story unfold vanish into thin air.

I stand back up, huffing with anger, stomping to the counter to catch my breath. I lean on the side, a pie I baked the other

207

day sitting nearby. I stare at it, the top a little too dark, the crust now too stale to be good.

I hear her rise from the creaky oak chair, and the hairs on my neck salute her, the loose skin on my arms chilling.

She struts across the kitchen, closing the gap between us calmly, slowly. I hear every footstep echoing, every slow, methodical footstep.

I've gone too far. Who do I think I am calling her on this? How stupid can I be to think I can rein in her danger? And now I've gone and prodded the beast and made myself vulnerable. My back to her, nobody here but me and her. I've made a terrible mistake, one I can't recover from now. It's too late to turn back. The monster is free to strike, and I'm at her mercy.

I've lived my life, and over the years, my fear of death has dulled. Perhaps it's the benefit of getting older, knowing death is knocking. You don't try so desperately to avoid it like you once did.

I'm not afraid to die, but I'm no martyr either. I carefully, slyly slide my hand towards the pie, the sharp knife I'd used to cut it resting casually in the pan. My fingers glide over the handle, and I grip it. The metallic handle feels familiar in my hand, and an energy seems to surge through me.

My heart rate calms and my mind clears.

'I'd back off if I were you,' she whispers in my ear, the warmth of her breath chilling my neck.

I don't move, the knife comfortably in my hand, the feel of it bolstering me. Suddenly, I'm not an elderly, frail lady waiting to die. Instead, with the feel of the knife, I'm transported back. I'm a young woman full of energy and vibrancy, ready to tackle the world. I'm the woman of my past, the don't-mess-with-me woman who commanded respect.

I'm fearless.

Her footsteps are again methodical as she crosses the kitchen, this time away from me. I don't turn around, staring at my hand on the knife handle as I hear her move down the entranceway. The door clicks shut — not a slam as one would expect. She's too confident, too cocky, to slam the door. She knows a gentle click is all she needs, that the soft gesture will make an impact.

I turn to the table, an empty wine glass sitting nakedly on the tabletop. I let go of the knife and cross the floor, rage boiling inside.

A rage I can't identify. A rage with roots stemming from a place I don't know.

I touch the cold glass, my fingers tracing an intricate pattern on it. And then, like a switch has been flipped in me, my hand grabs the bulb of the glass and slams it on the floor. The thousands of shards are a comfort to me as they fall in abstract patterns all around my feet.

Amos meowing at the window is the only thing that snaps me out of my trance, makes me remember what I've been wanting to forget.

It all makes so much sense now.

Chapter 28

The church bells tolled, the dinging chimes reverberating through the town that had been silenced by the freshly fallen snow. It was late afternoon on one of my favourite days – Christmas Eve.

Mom and Dad had allowed us to help pick out a tree last week, taking us deep in the woods to help cut it down. I'd picked a short tree, wide and plump. Of course, her choice had over-ridden mine, her ten-year-old cherubic grin and pointing finger irresistible to Mom and Dad. I tried not to think about it, tried to shove down the jealousy rising as we'd trudged through the snow, Dad lugging the evergreen behind him. I'd tried not to scowl as he wrapped an arm around her waist to boost her up so she could put the angel on the top.

She always got to put the angel on the top.

Church didn't start for a couple of hours, but we'd gotten dressed, knowing Mom would want us looking church-ready. I smoothed the front of my wrinkled gingham dress, the material scratchy, the popsicle stain on the bodice detracting from the velvet ribbon.

As I examined my hair in the mirror, fixing the unruly curls, she twirled in the corner of the room, her arms extended like a ballerina in the music box Great-grandma had given to me before she died. Around and around, she twirled, standing on her tiptoes in her perfectly shiny Mary Janes. Her dress was a gorgeous crushed red velvet, the lace bib on the front crisp and white, like the ground outside. The bow on the back was perfectly tied, and her braids hung gently around the collar. She looked like she could be the angel on top of the tree, her skin glowing with the luminescence of youthful joy.

My eyes burned at the sight of her, the perfection radiating off her. I glanced back at myself in the mirror, my two-year-old dress no comparison to the brand-new dress Mom had bought for her. It was who we were. She was the sparkling, pristine daughter, and I was the one left in the corner, tattered and ratty, forgotten and ill-fitting. She was twinkling, dazzling, and bright. I was dull and faded, stained by time and neglect.

I twisted my hands together, taking a deep breath to calm myself. It wouldn't do to get angry. It was my favourite day of the year, after all. Today, we'd sit as a family in the pew, listening to my favourite hymns, the church aglow with dozens of candles and the pungent smell of incense. I'd breathe deeply, the spicy scent filling my lungs, invigorating me.

There was something magical about Christmas Eve, something that made me feel ... hope. I felt like nothing bad could happen on Christmas Eve, like there was some kind of inexplicable ambiance in the air. And, despite everything, I felt like I was part of something bigger, sitting in that pew in the church celebrating something larger and more intricate than myself.

My sister and I wandered out to the kitchen where Mom was baking some last-minute cookies. I leaned on the frame of the window, staring out at the flying snowflakes.

It was breathtaking. Untouched beauty in its purest form.

'Mom, can we go outside and play in the snow?' my sister asked.

I turned. There was no way Mom would agree to that. She couldn't possibly say yes, not with us in our church clothes.

'Honey, it's almost time for church. You don't want to ruin your dress, do you? Plus, it's kind of cold out.'

'Please, Mom? It's so pretty out. Come on. We'll be careful.'

Mom turned to examine us, sighing. 'Just don't go far.'

My jaw almost popped open. She was letting us go? I couldn't believe it.

Still, I wasn't one to waste good fortune.

'Watch your sister,' Mom barked at me, pointing a finger as we both grabbed our snow boots and coats from the entranceway.

'Yes, ma'am,' I replied, suiting up for a snowy adventure.

* * *

'Mom said we shouldn't go far,' she whined as I led us deeper into the woods behind our house. I skipped through the snow, a light coating not enough to impede our travels. My dusty dress popped out from underneath my coat, the snowflakes catching on the scratchy material. I thought it was an improvement.

I ducked under some deadened tree branches, wandering into the forest behind our home. It was a place of imagination, of escape. When Mom let me out of the house, I loved to come back here, to explore, to pretend I was in a magical forest filled with fairies, wishes and things distant from the life I knew.

'Shut up, you baby. What, are you afraid?' I teased, out of earshot of the family. It felt good to mock her, to be harsh. Out here, with no one around, I could show my true feelings towards her.

'I'm telling when we get home,' she announced, her face shrivelled into the condescending expression I'd come to hate.

I seethed.

'Go ahead,' I replied, dashing further into the forest, hoping to leave her in the dust.

I shook off the annoyance that was my sister, trying not to let her get to me. She wouldn't ruin today. She wouldn't take away the magic.

We walked for a while until we reached the edge of the forest, my favourite place. The railway tracks ran through the woods, a juxtaposition of civilisation and nature that proved eerily pretty. Sometimes, especially in the summer months when school wasn't in session, I'd come here and stand, staring at the train when it flew by like clockwork, imagining what it would be like to jump on board, to ride off to a distant land. I wondered what it would be like to disappear, to vanish. I wondered if they'd even care, if they'd come looking for me.

I imagined hopping on the train, travelling to a faraway place where people were different. I daydreamed of finding a family who would buy me new dresses, who would applaud me for my imagination and hard work. I imagined going anywhere far away from here, far away from her.

I stood now, beside the track, my sister wandering up beside me, staring as well.

'What are we waiting for?'

I rolled my eyes. 'The train. It always comes through about now.'

'The train? Why would we want to watch a stupid train? You're so weird. No wonder Mom and Dad like me better.'

I turned then, the girl beside me not just a stranger, but a loathed enemy. Tears stung my eyes, not because of her words – but because of their truth.

We both knew she was right, but I hated hearing the words out loud. The embarrassment was too much.

I'd been here first. I was the first child in the family. I should be the one who was loved more. Why didn't they love me more?

It had all been fine until she came along, I convinced myself. For two years, I had been the pampered child, the loved child, the treasure. Okay, I couldn't remember a time without my sister, but it had to be true. It had to be her fault. It was all her fault.

I bit my lip, but I couldn't control the rage building. A deep, roaring hate roiled in my veins, coursing through my blood.

I hated her. I hated her smile and her sweet, gentle words. I hated the way she walked, the way she begged Mom and Dad and got her way. I hated her voice, her condescending glares, her elitist behaviour even at her young age.

I hated that she got the brand-new, red velvet dress while I wore the stained one. I hated that Mom and Dad kissed the ground she walked on while not even noticing I was on the ground at all.

I hated her, pure and simple. It was a smooth, strong hate that steadily increased with every single day.

'You bitch,' I bellowed as the train whistle blew, blasting through the forest and reminding us of its mighty strength.

And then, before I could think about it anymore, before I could weigh the consequences of what was about to happen, everything changed.

The train ploughed through the forest on its predestined track, blasting by, heading to a faraway land of my dreams, the guard probably distracted by some trivial thing. Maybe he, too, was lost in dreams that could never be. Or maybe he'd simply fallen asleep or turned his head. I'd never know.

But whatever it was, he didn't see the horrors unfold on the track. He didn't see the moment my dreams were tainted by a new vision as I stood, watching the black beast roar past. He *didn't see the girl, the girl who had once been my sister, oblit-erated by the heavy metal of the train, bits and pieces of her spewed across the quiet, beautiful landscape as I stood witness.*

When it was done, I stood alone, hands in the pockets of my ratty coat, wondering why I didn't feel a single thing.

Chapter 29

*L*ondon Bridge is falling down. Falling down.

Over and over, the words from my favourite childhood song play on repeat, the phrase chanting in my brain methodically as my big toe turns the tap on and off, on and off. The hot water is a contrast to the cold ceramic of the tub, my naked back chilling at the feel. I like it, though. I like the freezing-cold tub mixing with the shocking heat. I like the stinging, red skin it creates.

Falling down. London Bridge.

I used to sing it so many times as a child that my mother banned it in our house for a while. I don't know why, but I loved the song, the odd lyrics. The beauty of trapping the last, unsuspecting child in the clutches of the faux bridge, the single sacrificed child selected from so many to pay the price. The capture of the innocent between the squeezing arms.

My fair lady.

I think about the picture on the mantel, the roses surrounding us on that magnificent day, the day that would start my life on a new course. I think about the sacrifices made, and the sacrifices we didn't make.

Would I do it over again if I could? Or, if I could go back, if I could know what I do now, would I tell that woman standing in white by the rose bushes to run fast and never look back?

Christmas has come and gone, the tree at Bristol Lane dying a slow, tortured death before being baled into the front yard, a pile of dead needles. The winter has drudged forward, the iciness in the air finally breaking as spring pushes through. Soon, those beautiful rose bushes will be coming back in the front of the house. It's comforting, the predictability of it. Year after year, they come back. The roses will emerge from their long, long sleep, their thorns warding off any unwanted visitors. Their vibrant red hue will shine in the spring sun. I always love it when they come back. It's like a renewal, a reminder I've survived another season.

I do hope I live to see the roses come back.

I close my eyes, resting in the swirling water for a long time, Amos meowing at the edge of the tub. I splash him with some water to get him to shoo. I don't want my peace disturbed, not today.

It's been quite a few days, maybe even weeks, since Jane was here. Yet, I'm still buzzing from the encounter. True, it was an odd, uncomfortable confrontation. I should be upset about it. There's not much to celebrate when it comes to 312 Bristol Lane, that's for sure. But I don't feel upset. I feel a little bit empowered. I stood up to my neighbour. I reclaimed my fearless, courageous nature.

Most of all, I think I got through to her, because 312 Bristol Lane's been sort of quiet these days. I haven't seen any pushing or yelling. I haven't heard any screaming fights. Maybe I got through to her, finally.

I've won at last.

It's put me in a better mood, to tell you the truth. I even

took a break from the window yesterday to watch my soap operas and to rearrange the mantel, pulling his picture to the front. He stands in the front yard, those rose bushes in the background. He's got his jacket swung over his shoulder, a serious expression on his face. I'm pretty sure he's trying to be tough and stoic. It doesn't fool me. He's soft in the picture. He was always soft.

I took a long, hot bath yesterday too. It soothes my bones. I feel alive, so alive.

It's amazing what standing up to someone can do.

I finally emerge from the tub, pruny and more wrinkled than usual, and tuck myself into my clothes. I even stoop down to pull out the slippers I haven't worn in ages. I shrug, slipping them on my battered feet. I could use being pampered today. Who knows, maybe it'll even get warm enough this afternoon to wander out onto the front porch. Oh, maybe I'll make some tea and take Amos out there to watch the birds. He would like that. Where did he go after all? He's probably off licking his wet fur. I feel sort of bad now that I did that, but not really. He should have more manners, that cat. Couldn't he see I was relaxing?

Falling down. Falling down. I hum the tune as I casually stroll down the stairs, ignoring the pain in my hip and legs. I'll push through. I'm strong. I'm fearless. Who says I'm an old, washed-up—

And then it all goes black.

Chapter 30

My head is pounding. It's the first thought that rattles my brain.

It hurts so much, I don't even think I know where I am. And it's black. Everything is black, black, black.

I squint into the inkiness, trying to orient myself. There's a soft, fluffy texture against my cheek. Am I in bed? Did I go to bed?

No. Too hard to be my bed. And my legs and arms hurt way too much. I try to turn a little, but my hip screams in pain.

I slowly feel around with my right hand, trying to place myself.

I wriggle my toes, glad to see I can still do that. I feel something behind me, and now that I realise it, my head is against something hard. It's not a pillow.

And what's on my feet?

Slippers.

My eyes adjust to the darkness, and that's when I realise it.

The stairs. The slippers.

The damn slippers.

I've fallen.

My heart races. It doesn't do to fall at this age when you're home alone. Terror constricts my heart. My worst fear has happened. I'm doomed. I've seen the commercials. I know how this ends. And those little bracelet thingamajigs always seemed like extortion – until now. Now, I wish so badly I had one. Why didn't I buy one? All those times I worried about falling, I didn't think ahead enough to buy one of those bracelets. How could I have been so careless?

I take a deep breath, my head still aching. Amos is sitting beside me, and I do feel bad now for soaking him. How long have I been here? How long has it been since I fell?

I think back to the bathtub, to throwing water on Amos. It was morning. I was thinking about going outside.

And now it's dark, so dark without any lights on.

It must be night. I must've been here for a long, long time. My head is surging with pain. Am I bleeding? It's too dark to tell if there's any blood.

How much longer will I be here? How much longer until someone finds me? Panic races in my chest, my head aching and whirling as the fear rises up.

I'll be a dried-up, disintegrated carcase by then. Amos too. When there's no one to miss you, it's a pretty long time until you're discovered.

That feeling creeps in, and I try to shove it down but can't. Horror. Sheer horror.

I'm afraid. Not of death or dying, but of wasting away, powerless, here on the floor of my own home. How long until I starve to death or dehydrate? How long will it take?

A single tear trickles down my cheek, and I taste the saltiness.

I've got to get up. I have to pull myself up. I can do this.

I take a deep breath and focus on trying to sit up. I'm on my stomach, my cheek on the floor. My hip still throbs like there are a thousand knives in it. Is it broken? Are my legs broken?

It's hard to tell. I don't know anything anymore.

I take another breath and tell myself to count to ten. I do. And then I try to roll so that my arms are free. I need to get myself to my knees, need to prop myself so I can pull myself to my feet. That's all I need to do. I can do it.

I tell myself to focus, the darkness still surrounding me and making me nervous. But I have no choice. It's do or die, quite literally. I position myself so my hands are underneath my shoulders and get ready to do the most important push-up of my life. I was never good at push-ups. Fitness, brute strength, they weren't my strong suits. Still, left with no choice, I inhale until my lungs ache and I push with all my might.

My arms, flabby and underused, give out. It's a lot different lifting a cup of tea to your mouth versus lifting your entire upper body.

My lips touch the floor as I tumble back down, and I want to sob. My arms ache, and shifting has only hurt my hip more. I want to wallow in pity and scream at the unforgiving, merciless universe. But what good will that do?

Maybe this is how it ends, I think. And maybe it would serve me right. Maybe the universe isn't merciless — maybe it's completely just in its dishing out of punishment. I'll spend days in hell, alone, starving and thirsting and crying and hurting. Maybe this is the penance I've been heading towards all along. Maybe I'll pay the piper after all.

This saddens me at first, but then it angers me. There are plenty of people who have done horrible things and lived fine lives. Why do I have to pay? Why me?

Not me, I think. *I don't lose.*

So I try again.

And again.

My arms get weaker each time. They ache from the strain, and I'm no closer to getting up than when I started.

Breathless and exhausted, I cry out in frustration, scaring Amos away momentarily. Eventually, he comes back, though, the only trustworthy friend in my life.

Too bad he's going to die because of my wretched mistake.

I mix up my approach, deciding to try to roll to my side and kick my way up. I think about army crawling towards the sofa.

I turn myself around so my arms are on the stairs, thinking I can pull myself up. This goes on for what must be hours but feels like several eternities.

At some point, I drift off to asleep, exhaustion and fear mixing into a sleep-inducing potion. I know I may never wake up and although that terrifies me, it's also a relief. Sometimes, it feels good to just let go.

However, in the morning, when I open my eyes, my head still aching, I'm so happy to see the sight before me.

Help and hope have arrived – but it doesn't take long to realise it looks a lot different than I expected.

Chapter 31

'Thank God,' I proclaim through cracked lips. On my side, I look up at her towering over me. I didn't hear her come in. Then again, my head is killing me, and I've been lying on the floor for hours, almost a day probably. I'm hungry. I'm tired. I'm soiled.

I don't care how or when she came in. I'm just glad she's here.

She stands over me, arms crossed. She must be in shock.

'Help, please. I fell,' I annunciate, relief flooding over me as I state the obvious. She'll know what to do. She'll help. Despite everything, she's a good woman. I'm okay now. I'm going to be okay.

'I see that,' she replies, arms crossed. She shakes her head. 'What were you thinking?'

I take a laboured breath, wondering what she's doing. Can't we have this discussion later?

'I know, the slippers were stupid. I was careless. I swear, after this, I'm never going upstairs again. I don't think I've broken anything. But God, I hurt. I'm hurting so badly. Thank God I didn't take all those pain pills the doctor prescribed. I can get some after you help me up.'

My mouth practically waters at the thought of the sweet

relief in pill form. It will flood my veins with numbness, something I need more than ever now. It will quiet my screaming hip, my jagged joints.

I weakly lift a hand towards her, knowing this is going to hurt but thankful my ordeal will be over soon. Amos meows, still right beside me.

She scoffs at me and makes no move to grab my hand.

'You know I can't help you,' she says bitterly, smugly, the look on her face so condescending it enrages me. 'And he can't help you either.'

I'm in shock for a moment as she stares. 'What are you talking about? I know we've had our differences, but *please*. You know I don't have anyone. Please help me.' I hate hearing my own voice begging, but I'm desperate.

Surely, she's just toying with me. But I turn slightly so I can look up at her. She simply keeps grinning.

'You don't get it, do you? I *can't* help you. You have to help yourself.' There's a chilling calmness to her voice, a nonchalance that reveals her apathy towards the situation. Her calculated iciness is effective at revealing the harsh reality: she doesn't care what happens to me. She doesn't feel anything at all.

'Then why did you come over?' I ask.

She shrugs. 'Not sure, really. But listen, if you want to get out of this, figure it out. Or don't. It doesn't matter to me one way or another.'

And with that, she offers me a weak wave, turns on her heel, and leaves.

The door slams. Amos meows.

I want to cry. I want to rage. I want to kill her, in truth.

What kind of a woman does that? She's a true monster of

the most evil kind, getting pure pleasure from others' suffering. She's going to let me die here, let me rot away on my own floor. How can she live with herself? How can she possibly live with herself?

I shouldn't be surprised, after all I've witnessed. I'm not usually so naive. Still, for the months we've known each other, I've been lulled by the false pretences of a friendship between us, thinking that despite our differences, there was something there. I'd been fooled by the afternoon teas, the conversations, and Jane's sweet smiles. And, even when her behaviour sunk to all-time lows, even when the vilest side of her arose, I still believed somewhere deep within me that she was good. I'd believed in the possibility of salvation for her, of redemption. I'd had hope that the goodness in her, a goodness I'd detected on the first day, would usurp the evil.

But now I know I was wrong in the worst way, that there is no longer any hope for her. I know that any sense of friendship, of goodness, of possibility for her to start afresh is desecrated for good.

Rage boils and festers inside, a rage like I haven't felt in a while. It feels good, actually, to have it churning in me, through my blood. It gives my weak, failing body something to cling to.

She won't win. I'll show her.

Not only will I survive this and get myself out of this mess, but I'll also stomp over there and kill her myself.

She's not getting away with this.

And it is because of my anger that I find a new resolve. I take a few deep breaths and count to ten. I order myself to think, to find the logical answer. I can't get up, not in this position. But that doesn't mean I have to do nothing.

I pull myself inch by inch into the living room, my body screaming the entire way. Hours tick by, my throat aching for water. My arms shake with effort, and every millimetre is equivalent to a mile. But I'm stubborn when I need to be, and I'm no quitter. No one, no one is getting one up on me.

I'm pretty sure a day goes by before I get myself to the sofa. Glancing at the prominently displayed picture of him on the mantel, I find an inner strength from deep within. It's spooky, really.

And finally, by some miracle or sheer will to beat her, I've pulled myself up on the sofa and am resting on my back, catching my breath.

Miracle among miracles, I reach into the end table nearby and find the pain pills prescribed weeks ago from the doctor. I pop a few and drift off to sleep, knowing tomorrow isn't going to be much easier.

But, in a strange way, I'm thankful. Because, in the end, whether she wanted to or not, she saved me after all.

Chapter 32

Playing in the forest … terrible tragedy … didn't see the child on the tracks … too young.

The words spun around me as I stood in my black dress that was one size too small and three holes in the bottom too worn.

The snow and wind howled in a cacophony of chaos out the window as I watched, strangers and family members wandering about our home, coating every inch of it.

The snow had been so cold, and the rose had been so red against the casket.

That was all I could remember.

It was such a waste to have a casket. There was nothing left of the mangled body to put in there, after all. She'd been splattered, her blood red against the dusting of snow, a contrast not unlike the rose on the casket. It had been so pointless. Why had they even bothered?

In truth, it hadn't sunk in yet. It was just me now. It was only me. Maybe it was because of the lack of a body, the lack of closure. She was there one minute and then gone the next. She had, like in my daydreams, truly disappeared, the train taking her to a distant land none of us would visit in this lifetime. I wondered if she was in a happy place. Despite the priest's words about her innocence and how she was being received by

God, I couldn't be sure. Life here was too hard for me to believe in an afterlife of serenity and peace. I didn't know what that would feel like.

People I didn't know surrounded my parents, my mother sobbing into a handkerchief already soaked with tears. Dad stood, stoic as always, a tie around his neck for the first time. He'd taken to carrying a photograph of her in his left hand, like some token he couldn't put down.

I stared out the window, the driveway filled with cars. I glanced towards the kitchen, the array of casseroles dotting the counter an overwhelming mess.

It was too much. It was all too much.

After the train had flown by, I'd slogged home, feeling dead and tired.

It had taken a while for them to notice I was alone. They'd asked me questions, had demanded I take them to the tracks, panic ensuing. Mom ran like she could get there in time, like she could change things. Dad grabbed my arm, squeezing it too tight the entire way.

But it was too late. I told them it was too late.

There was nothing left of her but a smattering of blood and remnants of her skin, her organs splattered about the snow. It had been going too fast. The train hadn't even stopped. Had the train driver noticed the tiny girl in her bright red coat? Had the world noticed? Had I?

Over and over, the tale was retold. How she'd wanted to play by the tracks. How I'd begged her to come home. How the train had snuck up, no whistle, no warning. How I'd tried to grab her, but it was too late.

Over and over, I told the story. Over and over, I dulled the guilt, the pain, the sadness that tried to well up. It wasn't my

230

fault. I swore to them over and over it wasn't my fault. I told myself it wasn't my fault.

For the first day or two, I was racked with confusion. I'd ceaselessly replayed the scene in my exhausted mind, but all I could conjure up was the conversation we had before and the sight of the train after. The in-between was a black hole swallowing up every remnant of memory. Why couldn't I remember?

Then again, maybe I did remember. Maybe I just didn't want to.

'Darling, come into the kitchen. Have a bite to eat. You've been through so much.' The words of the neighbour lady startled me. I turned to look at her kind face, seeing a warmth I haven't experienced in a long time. I was thankful for her willingness to care for me. My parents couldn't even stand to look at me since the accident let alone make sure I was eating. I knew they associated me with her death. However, I also recognised the dark truth unspoken: they wished it had been me who had died instead of Lucy. I was the daughter who came back, the daughter no one favoured. I should have been the one to die. I wouldn't have been missed.

They would give anything for it to have been me instead of her.

The neighbour lady set a plate in front of me, touching my shoulder with a tenderness foreign to me. Mom and Dad were tucked away, Mom in the bedroom and Dad talking to the strangers who had filled our house in the period of mourning, offering unsolicited opinions and meek attempts at comforting words.

Mom and Dad, though, walked around in a silent stupor, the pain apparently deadening their ability to speak. I hadn't heard their voices for days. In fact, the last thing Mom said to me was,

'How could you let this happen? How could you have let our precious baby die?' Since those words, she'd only managed sobs.

Playing with the bland tuna casserole on my plate, I sat in silence as well, wondering if my parents would ever speak to me again.

And, for the rest of the day, I sat at the table, stuffing my face with food, realising I was all alone now – and wondering if that was such a bad thing, silence and all.

Chapter 33

An ageing, ailing body doesn't heal quickly. I think about calling an ambulance the next morning when I pop a few more pain pills and drag myself to the kitchen. I'm desperately thirsty and hungry, so I take care of those needs. My hips, legs, back and head are all stiff, but the painkillers ease the dreadful aches. I find a half-empty bottle of wine on the counter and take a swig.

Nothing's broken. Maybe my bones are so flimsy that there was nothing to break. Or maybe it was some kind of miracle, I don't know. But I survived. Against all the odds, I'm still here.

I don't know how I feel about that, in truth. Breaking my neck on those stairs would've been an easy way to go. In some ways, it would have been easier to be at the end of this life of hardship, to not have to think anymore. I'm so tired, and not just from the fall. However, I'm still here, so I guess there's no use in wishing it was over. The day will come, soon enough I'm sure, but not today. Not now. And so, I must trudge on again, as I've done for so long.

I need to clean myself up, take care of some hygiene, but I'm too weary, and to be honest, I'm too terrified to face those stairs again. I'll tend to my needs later, when I've cooled my nerves.

After another swig of wine, I make my way to the window. I stare out at 312 Bristol Lane for the first time since the accident, thinking about it all. The decline, the sunshine-yellow woman who has all but disappeared. I think about her standing over me, about how she refused to help.

I think about how I want to hate her, how I want to get revenge – and yet, how I oddly understand.

Maybe I'm the one losing it. Of course, alcohol, painkillers and a potential concussion will probably do that to a person. Besides, even if I want revenge, I don't think my limp and tortoise-slow speed would do me much good.

So, instead, I sit down in my favourite spot, rocking gently so as not to jar my bones. I look out the window, the sun shining softly through the clouds. Spring. A time of renewal, of rebirth. Despite my near-death experience, I don't really feel anything like renewal. I feel like death, in reality.

It all looks the same, which makes sense. Of course it would look the same. Nothing has changed. Then again, it feels like everything is different. It seems almost eerie that there is no outward sign of the internal transformations and mutations that have occurred. It's unsettling that the same picturesque building is housing what I now understand to be evil. I wonder if she's been thinking about me. I wonder if she thinks I'm dead. Well, the joke's on her. I'm still here. I'm still witnessing.

And witness I do.

Chapter 34

Fragile. Frail. Breakable. These are not the words one would associate with her – but today, I do. She's changed again. She's weaker somehow. She looks like she's the one who fell down the stairs.

It is this feebleness, though, that terrifies me the most. I'm running out of time. I feel it in my lungs, in my chest, in the recesses of my inner being.

I need to do something. I need to save him. I need to save us all.

This whole thing has gone too far, and I've sat witness too long. So many excuses have swirled in my head, a jarring carousel tune that won't stop. I need to stop it. I have no choice but to stop it because suddenly, with clarity, I realise how this thing ends – and I can't let it happen.

* * *

She sits now in the dining room, staring out the window. For a long moment, I wonder if she's staring at me – but then I realise her face is too blank, too forlorn to be making a statement. She's too far gone.

She rests, hands perched on the arms of the chair, gaze

steadily fixed on – what? The sky? The birds? The grass? – for hours. I stare right back, studying, watching, waiting.

What's going on in that head of hers? Is tonight the night she pushes it too far?

No. She's too fragile today. She's not feeling powerful today. She's ... different. Almost pathetic.

Her body is slumped so that she's almost folded into herself, and I see the crumpling of her body as a mirror image of the crinkled soul within.

How does one get so lost? And why isn't anyone trying to pull her out?

Desperation clings in my chest. Why couldn't I pull her out? What was I thinking? Instead of helping, I've pushed her. The knife. The harsh words. The questioning statements.

I knew better. I know better. That was my chance. I could've set things right. I could've made up for it all. But now it might be too late.

It's all too late, but the thing is, I did know. I knew.

And it's the fear in me that's been fighting back, sinking its teeth into her, into the situation, and into everything else around me.

* * *

I inhale sharply as my eyes fling open, my heart racing. Before I can understand what's happening, I see her wicked grin, her almost-black eyes. Her pupils are too large, and her skin is milky grey.

She stands over me now, silent. I sit straight up, scooching so my back is against the headboard, the sheet still pulled over my legs as I inch my bottom closer to the lumpy pillow.

Heart pumping and breath ragged, I feel tears welling.

I push them back down. This is no time to cry. I need to be reasonable. I need to be cunning. I need to survive.

He needs me to survive.

'Please,' I say gently. It's not a begging word the way I say it. It's a calm, rational word that asks her to reconsider.

But hovering over me, she's too calm now, too rational as well. Her ruby-red lips don't utter a single word or explanation, they just curl upwards into a smile, disconcerting.

How did she get in here?

Now that the veil of sleep is lifting and the panic of the shock has dulled enough for thoughts to come in, it's the question of the moment. How did she get in here? And what does she want?

I don't have to study her long to know what she wants can't be good.

The darkness drowning out my room is partially broken up by the moonlight cascading through the window. The beam of light glints off the item in her right hand, the shimmer mesmerising.

The knife. She's got a knife.

I take two deep breaths – I don't have time for ten. Not now.

I don't move a muscle, afraid of triggering her.

'What do you need?' I ask, fighting to keep my voice soothing.

I fight to hold back the scream gurgling in my throat. What good will it do though to scream? Who will hear me?

She says nothing, her uncanny smile still painted on her face. I don't even think she blinks as she creeps forward, her feet plodding on the carpet, thudding towards me. I scamper to the edge of the bed, my fingers now clutching the sheet.

This is how it all ends. This is where I leave this world. This is where my chance to change things cracks.

I bite my lip so hard I taste blood. I don't squeeze my eyes shut. I need to see her, to look into the face of the woman sacrificing me. If this is how I go, I'm determined to face the end with dignity, with grace and with the knowledge that atonement is now mine.

But right before the knife can plunge into my chest, before the hot blood can cascade down my chest in a final dance, before the sweet release can absolve me from the lifetime of horrors, my eyes flash open.

Panting, heart pounding, I stare up at the ceiling, the sheet up to my chin.

I sit up with a start, eyes darting across the room.

Nothing. No one.

Just empty blackness, no moonlight, no Jane from 312 Bristol Lane, no knife.

Just me and the emptiness again. Always me and the emptiness.

I take ten deep breaths and bite my lip, the taste of the blood comforting in the silent darkness.

Chapter 35

His picture sat in the frame in front of me, but I couldn't see it. The darkness suffocated me.

Then again, I never really could breathe those days. I'd grown used to not breathing.

The funeral, the casseroles, the smell of flowers that burned my nose — it had all been a whirling yet familiar blur. I didn't remember the words of comfort spoken at the service. I didn't remember what I wore. I didn't remember being alive. In truth, I don't think I wanted to be alive. He was gone. He was dead. He wasn't there.

And it was all my fault.

No one knew, of course. Just like before, I'd managed to fool them all. It was almost laughable how trusting people could be, how naive. I'd learned that early on in life. After all, people only see who and what they want to see.

Tears fell and pity collected in their eyes as they studied me. Poor thing, they thought. All alone.

They blamed him. They talked about how selfish he was, how unreasonable to leave his wife all alone. Some talked of him with pity. They talked of pain and how they didn't know.

But how could they have known? No one could have known. Except me. I knew.

Because it was my fault. I did this. I pushed too far, once again.

The rage, the anger – it was unstoppable.

What was wrong with me?

And so, there I sat, alone in the world once more, just darkness surrounding me and a house of memories that had gone cold.

All those regrets swirled over and over and over in my head. All those horrid scenes played out. All those biting words. All those vicious accusations. All those shoves and outbursts and uncontrollable fits of rage.

The knife in my hand, up against his throat. His words that pushed me and pushed me, that made me so angry. The deep depressions, the horrible feelings of moroseness. The empty womb, the empty life, the empty heart.

It's my fault, I thought, because, even then, I knew.

I knew I would live with my actions for the rest of my life. Would live with the guilt for the rest of my life.

And the monster inside of me roared its head, told me it wasn't over. It wasn't finished yet.

There was something seriously wrong with me. But the worst part of it? I was completely and utterly alone with my seriously scarred, flawed self. I would be my only company. From the moment I pushed him too far, it was just me, my regrets and the knowledge that everything that had happened, everything that would happen, was because of me.

And so I sat for a long time, night after night, in a darkness that plagued me, hoping it would help me find some peace. But, as I found out too late, peace never, ever comes for the weary, the weak or the marred.

Chapter 36

A new development greets me in the morning.

My eyes are heavy, craving sleep, but I know I have my duty. I don't even make tea. I scrape a few chunks of tuna into Amos's dish before rushing to my chair, my body heavy on the seat today. I don't even feel like rocking.

My gaze darts around the property, taking inventory, taking note.

Things are definitely different.

Her suitcases are on the front porch. Two large, red suitcases, impressive in size and in the statement they are making.

I put a hand to my mouth. What's she doing? What is she thinking?

In some ways, I wonder if I should turn around, should let her go. He would be better off without her. I should return to my days of watching the soap operas, drinking tea and waiting to die. Life was easier before Jane and Alexander Clarke moved in. It took me some time to see that. But things would be easier for me and for Alex, too, if Jane left. He would learn to live life without her dangerous wrath. From what I've observed, which has been a lot, he's a kind man. He's a good man. Even at her lowest, at her darkest, he's stood by her. He's shown her nothing but patience and love. I've never seen a streak of violence in him, even in retaliation. I've never seen anything concerning. I've seen nothing but love. Naive, foolish love, but love all the same.

What's his story? What drives him to stay? What could possibly have dented him in the past so that he can't stand up to her?

But I know what it is. I've experienced the thing holding him back first-hand – love.

Sure, love is beautiful and breathtaking. It makes life worthwhile. That's something I can say for certain in my lonely house, the faded wallpaper surrounding me in an empty cocoon. I know what it is to love and to be without love. I know it's what drives life forward, what makes us feel alive. But I also know it's what sometimes holds us back, what blinds us to reality. It brainwashes us into believing that without love, we are nothing. It shields us from the truth, from what's best for us sometimes.

He loves her, plain and simple. Long curls, short curls, sweet smile, or raging temper, he loves her. Whatever it is that holds them together, it's strong, at least for him. Because even as she rages like a wild storm, he loves her. I see it in his gentle touch when she's whaling on him, in the pain in his eyes as he's begging her to stop.

He's a victim – of her, of circumstance, but mostly of love.

I can't judge him for what he's put up with because I know that love is strong. It's not always wise. It's not always rational. Sometimes it just is, even when we don't want it to be.

So as I see her wander out and sit on the suitcase, staring out into the street, I think that maybe I should let her go. This could be the start of something new for both of them.

I wish her well. I hope she finds herself, finds peace, finds happiness. I hope she finds a cure to the madness that must be quaking inside.

But as I touch the window, studying the beautiful blonde, something in me cracks. Like him, I'm drawn to her. I can't give up on her. Maybe I can change this. Maybe she just needs me to help change this. I know what it's like to give up on yourself, to give up on the life you thought you could have. So a part of me still, against all odds, wants to believe I can change this. I want to believe that even though it isn't the easiest path, it's still possible. That she isn't the lost cause I've come to believe. As ridiculous as it sounds, I still want to be right about the goodness I once saw in her, in them. I want her to realise she can change.

This is no time to be a coward. This is the time to step up, to be brave, and to do the right thing, something I haven't always done in the past.

I gently put Amos on the floor and laboriously lift myself from the wooden seat, shuffling towards the door. It's a drizzly morning, but I don't bother grabbing a coat or a hat. I just open the door and greet the morning, hoping that maybe the fog will lift.

I carefully trudge out onto the porch, and she looks up. I wave to her.

'Morning. Can you come over?' I yell across the street.

She stares for a long moment as if in contemplation, her head tilted. Her eyes study me as if I'm an apparition, as if she wasn't expecting to see me. Perhaps after the stairs situation she wasn't. I shove the thought aside. I need to focus on other things now. I need to focus on helping her.

She's got a bandana tied in her hair and a raincoat on, a

243

yellow raincoat. She looks so different from the stunning beauty who moved in, even though she's still beautiful in her own right.

She doesn't say a word, but silently rises from the suitcase, crossing the yard with purpose and grace. I sit down on the ledge of the porch, balancing myself carefully. She comes over and stands before me.

'Hey,' she says, her voice weak and scratchy.

'Hi,' I say.

There's a defiance about her this morning. I can feel it in the way she stands before me as I sit. I can see it in her eyes blazing with something new. I don't know what it is even though it feels familiar.

'Where are you going?' I ask gently, no judgement in my voice.

'I don't know yet. But away. I need to get away.'

'Why?' I ask. The questions are simple, but I've found that sometimes all someone needs is to be asked the simple questions.

She sighs. 'It's complicated.'

'So explain it.'

'I don't know. It's just – this. I know we can't keep going like this. He's not the man I signed on for. He's not the man I married.'

'I see,' I say, even though I don't, not really. Because if anyone got duped in marriage, I feel like it's him. Still, I try to reserve judgement. Judgement isn't what she needs now. It isn't going to help. 'Look, I don't want to meddle, believe me. But I've learned a thing or two over the years about life, love, regrets. I'm not an expert, truly. I'm the first to admit I've made plenty of mistakes. But maybe that's why I feel like I need to speak up. I need to warn you, maybe, so someday you're not sitting here like me. Because, let me tell you, when you get to my age, you have too much time to sit and think about your regrets. Way too much time. I'm hoping I can save you some of that pain.'

'You think I'm making a mistake,' she says assuredly, a statement of fact rather than a questioning observation. She is placid, as if it doesn't matter anymore. It's the voice of a woman who has checked out in every single way.

'I think you're making a lot of mistakes.'

'I see.' She bites her lip and looks off into the distance.

'Look, I don't want to make you mad. But you have to believe me. I see you. I do. I see your pain and your fear. I know you're not happy, but I also know leaving won't make it better. You'll just spend your life running from whatever this is. You need to confront it. You need to change. You need to find happiness in the life you have. You need to stop blaming him for everything you didn't get. He loves you. He really loves you. And maybe he's not perfect. Maybe this life isn't perfect. But it could be so much worse. Truly.'

'What, it could be yours?' she asks. It sounds harsh, but I know she doesn't necessarily mean it that way. I get it. I'm not offended.

'In a way, yes. But I also mean it could be worse if you leave and realise someday that this is actually what you needed all along. Look, life is hard. I know you've been through a lot. I can see in your eyes that you carry a lot of pain. When you first moved in, I thought you were all sunshine and smiles, but I know now that was a cover. I know life's not perfect for you, but I also know you control so much of it. Think about him. Think about what you have before it's too late.'

245

'I'm tired. I'm tired of feeling trapped. I won't let him trap me. He's not keeping me here. Did you know he thinks I need help, like professional help? He wanted me to go to the hospital. It's not happening. I'm not going to be some medical experiment. I'm not going to let him shove me away so he can go off and screw every woman I know he's looking at. I won't let him make a fool out of me. No one makes a fool out of me.'

Tears well in her eyes.

I reach for her hand, but she pulls away. She's gone, so far gone.

It feels hopeless.

But I try one more time. This is so important. 'I know what it feels like to be trapped, an endless cycle of hell playing over and over. I know what it's like to be afraid. But, honey, he loves you. I don't think he wants to lock you away or trap you. I think he wants you to be happy. I don't know how you get there. Maybe you need help. Maybe you don't. Maybe you just need a new perspective. Maybe you need to figure it out for yourself. Maybe you need to learn to control your anger. I don't have all the answers. I do, however, have an idea of what this path you're following could turn out like. Safe isn't always the enemy. Sometimes safe and simple is what we need. Please think about it.'

She wipes a single tear from her eye, sighing.

'Okay. I will,' she says.

She nods, puts her hands in her pockets, and heads back across the street. I turn to watch her lug the suitcases inside. I breathe a sigh of relief.

I know she needs help, more help than a few words from an old lady like me can offer. Still, it's a start. Maybe this will change things. Maybe together they can fix this. Maybe all hope isn't lost.

I sit for a long time, the misty fog settling on Bristol Lane, shielding my view of the house. I don't need to see in today, though. I just need to cross my fingers that an awakening is happening, that things are going to change and that it isn't too late.

It's never too late for hope, I think, as I head back inside, feeling warm for the first time in a long time.

Chapter 37

*E*ven in death, she was still winning. She was still the favourite.

I sat in my room, alone, my parents doing whatever it was they did. The funeral had been over for weeks, the casseroles devoured. I thought the pain would dull, that life would go on. They still had me, after all. Life had to go on.

But I was wrong. Life didn't go on, not without her. It never would.

I ambled inside now, slinging my backpack to the floor, and glanced around the kitchen, the dead flowers from the funeral still sitting in the centre of the table, a monument to their favourite daughter, a reminder of what had been lost.

'I'm home,' I called warily, not a sound to be heard.

No one responded. I shuffled into the living room, where Mom slept on the couch, her position most days since the accident. If she wasn't there, she was tucked away in her bedroom. Dad had instructed me to leave her alone. He wasn't there now, probably at McGulliver's Inn down the street. He'd been spending more and more time there.

And I'd been spending more and more time alone.

They couldn't look at me.

They blamed me.

On the day after the funeral, when the shock had dulled and the immediacy of the situation had resolved itself, it became clear they could never forgive me.

'What the hell were you doing? Why didn't you save her?' Dad bellowed out of nowhere as we sat, silent, in the living room the next night, the darkness enveloping us except for the single lamp.

'I couldn't. It was too fast,' I muttered, dread gripping my heart.

'You lying bitch,' he said, stomping towards me as I cowered on the chair.

My cheek stung as his hand made contact with it, his large, calloused hand a powerful surge against my face. Tears welled in my eyes, not from the physical pain, but from the fact that even now, she was winning.

Even now, without her to steal the spotlight, I was nothing.

I couldn't win. I'd never win.

I walked past Mom, who was snoring lightly on the couch. I tiptoed to my room, not wanting to have to deal with her. I shut my door, tucked into my safe zone in the world — at least until Dad got home.

I sat on my bed, pulling my knees to my chest, rocking gently.

Why wasn't I good enough? Would I ever be good enough?

Rocking back and forth, I made myself promise not to cry. I wouldn't break down. I wouldn't let her win. I would grow strong from this. I would rise up. And someday, when I left this place, I'd leave her memory behind for good.

I wouldn't let anyone get the best of me. I wouldn't let anyone win.

I would be the winner, someday. I just had to be strong enough to outlast this suffering and then I could be victorious after all.

Chapter 38

She leaves on a Tuesday, late morning. I watch the taxi whip into the driveway, observe her stuffing her suitcases into the back. She stands for a moment, longingly studying 312 Bristol Lane before she climbs into the taxi and leaves the house behind.

And just like that, she's gone. Her sunshine-yellow promises, her ugly episodes, her atrocious threats.

I take a deep breath, but I don't feel relief.

I don't feel like things are going to get better. No, I know things aren't going to get better.

That night, I dream of knives. Rooms full of knives, blood dripping. I dream of drowning in blood, my lungs heaving for oxygen as I'm slipping down, down, further into the blood.

When I awake that night and come to, I realise I'm holding something.

A knife.

I've been sleeping with it under my pillow the past few nights. I've felt this need to be able to protect myself, stirring from somewhere deep within. Maybe it's all the horrible memories flooding back. Maybe it's the fact that I still don't know what she's going to do, that she's unpredictable. Or maybe I just like the feel of it close like I had once before.

Sitting up in bed, I look down to see a trickle of blood from a gash in my palm where I must've held the knife too tight.

I don't drop it. I don't go to get a bandage. I just squeeze it a little harder, the sharp burn in my hand bringing relief.

* * *

One day. She's been gone one day.

It's Wednesday now, but his car's still in the driveway. He didn't go to work today. I wonder if he's mourning her or celebrating. I can't be certain.

Without her at home, I find the window a lot duller. There's not much to see. He doesn't scamper about like she did. Plus, without her there, I don't feel the burden of needing to constantly watch. In a sick way, I miss it.

Maybe I'm the twisted one.

I busy myself making some soup – chicken, my favourite. I take a hot bath. I turn on the soap operas. But nothing interests me. I find my mind leaping, wandering. This can't really be how it all ends, can it? How pointless would that be? What could the purpose of all this possibly be?

It's anticlimactic. In a good way, of course. But still, it's anticlimactic.

Even the soap operas do a better job.

Mostly out of boredom, I wander to the door around one in the afternoon. The sun is shining. I crack open the door, thinking about sitting outside on the porch. Maybe I'll put Amos in his harness. He does hate the trapped feeling, but the sunshine is so good for him, I know. We all need to be trapped now and then for our own good, right?

I'm fiddling with the mailbox when I feel something brush my leg. I look down to see a ball of fur rushing onto the porch.

'Amos!' I shout, tossing the mail down and opening the door wider, beckoning the cat back in. But he's too interested in the little bird that's hopping on the lawn. 'Amos, come back,' I yell, stumbling onto the front porch now, panicked.

Amos keeps scampering, chasing the bird across the road.

He's fast, too fast. I'll never make it over there. And I can't lose Amos. Not now. Not ever.

Tears well as I beg my old legs to cooperate. I manoeuvre the steps, trying to keep an eye on my beloved cat as I do. It's not easy. I'm so afraid of falling again. At least this time, it'll be outside and maybe someone will find me.

I look up to see the door to 312 Bristol Lane open. Alex's keys are in his hand, but he looks up and catches my eye. He sees me on the steps and, as if by a miracle, Amos pauses in the lawn right before getting to 312 Bristol Lane.

I hurry down the steps, afraid of falling but more afraid of losing my beloved friend. The cat, momentarily frozen by the sight of the bird, sits still. Within seconds, I snatch Amos in my arms. He meows and claws as I clutch him tightly.

'Stupid cat. I don't know what I'd have done if you'd have gotten away.'

I start heading towards my porch, but I turn to see that Alex is still standing at his car, staring at me. He nods, and

I stop in my tracks, studying him for a long moment. I've seen him so many times, but for some reason, today, I see him differently. I realise something I haven't taken time to note. He's so ... handsome. He looks so handsome. So sweet.

I've looked at this face over and over from my seat at the window. I've watched him go to his car every morning. I've watched him with Jane, through the window, on the front porch. But now, I realise none of that did him justice.

My heart palpitates as those icy blue eyes study me. He smiles, not just from his mouth, but with his eyes.

Peace floods me all over again. But then, he climbs into the car, cautiously.

Where is he going?

I scamper up the stairs, Amos slung over my shoulder. I pause before the door, watching the car peel out.

Is he headed into town? Maybe he's going to the bus station to see if he can find her. Maybe he still hasn't given up.

I bet that's it. He's the kind of man to do that, the kind who cares so much he'd chase her down. He thinks maybe he can find her. I bet he thinks he can still fix things.

I consider running after the car, stopping him. I want to tell him he's crazy, that he should let her go. I think about spilling my soul to him, about how you can't help someone that far gone, about how he needs to get himself out. I want to tell him he's breaking and not realising it, that even here in the spring sunshine I can see a dejectedness, a melancholy that's unhealthy in him. She's wearing him down, grinding him down, yet he's too blind to see it.

All of these words and phrases dance on my tongue. I want to apologise for not helping him sooner. I want to confess that I want to help him. I want to say I'm sorry for sitting by and watching him break. I want to beg him to get out, to find himself help, to abandon her. She's a lost cause at this point. I know that — why doesn't he? Why can't he see that? Why is he too good of a man, of a husband, to just write her off?

But thinking about those icy blue eyes, I know with finality nothing will work. I can't get through to him. You can't help someone who won't help themselves. You can't help the completely lost. You can't change what's already been set into motion.

'I wish you the best of luck,' I murmur into the emptiness, his car long gone, Amos still struggling in my arms. I stand tall, willing myself to feel a strength and confidence I don't feel right now.

I think about how there's something between us. A camaraderie in the misery. A connection in the fear. A knowledge of what we share, perhaps. A mutual understanding of what she is and how it will be. A pity — for her, for us, for the world.

I stare at 312 Bristol Lane for a long, long time after setting Amos inside my own house.

I stand long after the car has pulled out of the driveway, long after the house sits empty.

I stand long after I have my chance to do something about it all.

Finally, I go inside. Amos is curled up on the couch after his afternoon adventure.

I sit beside him, staring at the picture on the mantel, and I cry.

I cry because I know all too well what it's like to lose someone and to want desperately to find them again. I know all too well what it's like to grasp at straws, to grasp at what-ifs and to grasp at time that can't be reclaimed.

Snot bubbling from my nose so thick that I can't breathe, I gulp in air, rising from my seat and crossing the living room with a purpose I haven't felt in ages.

My fingers graze the cracked glass, a layer of dust grimy to the touch. I stare at the rose bushes, the picture of us, the painted-on smiles behind the jagged pieces.

London Bridge is falling down.

I wipe a streak clean on the glass, and then cross over it, an 'X' marking the spot.

Falling down.

With two hands, I clutch the photograph in my hands, stepping back from the mantel, tears blurring my vision until we're just fuzzy black-and-white blobs behind a fragile protective screen.

Falling down.

I stare at the floor when it's done, the shards dancing around my feet in a dazzling display of complexity.

I crouch down, sitting among the crumbling pieces, my finger tracing the patterns on the hardwood floor for a long time.

When I've mastered the pattern, I stand, heading to the rocking chair. I rock. Back and forth. Back and forth. *London Bridge is falling down.* Creak. Creak. Creak. Creak.

I don't know how long I rock for, the tears drying to my face. But by the time the sun comes up in the east, the car is pulling back into the driveway and my calves scream in pain from the rocking motion.

He slams the door and trots up the stairs hurriedly, as if he doesn't want anyone to see him.

I see him. I want to scream that I see him as he heads into the lonely house silenced by the lack of her.

But I don't think it matters if I see him.

Life isn't always about seeing.

Then again, sometimes it is.

Chapter 39

Sometimes I wish I'd been the one to disappear.

I don't want to be here. I can't be here.

It's the mantra I'd chanted over and over, at too many stages in life. The words were a razor-thin shard of glass against my wrist, close enough to create a burning pain but not close enough to sear through my purple, pulsing veins.

I picked at a green ball of fuzz on the edge of my tattered quilt, my fingers deftly pulling at the stubborn sign of wear. My back against the headboard of my bed, I thought about sitting there all day like I had so many times before, lost in the little piece of both heaven and hell I wallowed in so frequently.

She deserved it. She started it.

After all that time, after all those years, I'd come to that conclusion.

It wasn't my fault because she deserved it. She started it.

They pushed me to it. All of them pushed me to it.

Still, despite the years that had passed, I couldn't let it go. They wouldn't let me. I danced in a limbo-like state of the past, of the present and of a future of unending days of forced penance.

My chest burned as I spun the fuzz I'd plucked from the blanket over and over between my fingers. I stared blankly at the wall as I did, wondering if I could sit in my desolate room until I disappeared, wondering how long until they'd notice.

Weeks? Months? Years? Would they even notice at all?

Who was I kidding, though?

Six years. That's how long I'd really been gone. Six years they'd continued mourning her, or more accurately worshipping her. Her death only heightened their love for her, their reverence. It only detracted from their feelings for me.

Her death hadn't lifted me up to a new status in the family. Instead, I was even more overshadowed by her silhouette, by her ashen shell, by her spectre that haunted the house via memories, photographs and what-ifs.

She was dead, but she still commanded more respect than I did. It hurt to be second fiddle to a skeleton.

I rocked back and forth on my bed like I'd done for so many days, so many nights. I'd grown accustomed to being alone, had even perhaps grown to accept it.

But my days of being a prisoner in that house were coming to an end. I was getting older, and opportunities would present themselves soon. I just had to hang in there. I just had to survive. And then I'd get my chance to be free, to rise up, to be noticed. I would command respect. I would command to be noticed.

No one would ever again ignore me. No one would get the better of me. No one would keep me down.

My chest burned with what, I didn't know.

Someday, I told myself, someday I'd find someone to cling to, someone to notice me.

Someday, I'd find someone who didn't see me as second best. And when I found that someone, I'd clutch them so tightly, so fiercely, that they wouldn't have a chance to let go of me.

They wouldn't have a chance to smash me into ruins on the floor, scattered pieces centred around a sanctuary for someone else.

Someday, it would be my turn to be at the top.

Chapter 40

Six days.

Six days and thirteen hours, but who is counting? Me. I'm counting.

I'm drifting off at the window, creak creak, rock rock. The sound of screeching brakes startles me as the yellow taxi door flings open. She tugs on her red suitcases, shoving them in the driveway. The taxi leaves, and she stands, in the same outfit she left in.

She readjusts her scarf for a moment as she stares at the house.

I perk up. She's back.

Clearly, despite all odds, she's come to her senses. I hate myself for feeling hopeful again, but I'm desperate for it. No matter how many times she proves that she's completely gone, I can't help but think she's going to get it right. I can't help but feel like this will be the time it will be different.

This is going to be different, better now. She wouldn't have come back otherwise, right? What would've been the point?

But when she turns towards me, staring into the window, I know she's staring at me. I lock eyes with her, and her lips curl up in the grin, the familiar smirk I saw once before.

When she was standing over me in my room, the knife in her hand.

It was just a dream, I remind myself. A nightmare. It meant nothing.

But she stands tall, proud. Her head is too high. She might be wearing the same outfit, but she's changed. There's a gully between who she was six days and thirteen hours ago and who she is now. There's something different about her.

She's not scared anymore. She's not down.

She's – dare I say – confident?

Dad always said a scared dog was the most dangerous, but I don't know. I don't think he knew about Jane Clarke when he said that.

Because as she struts up the driveway, wheeling two suitcases behind her, there's something in her walk that's terrifying. There's something in her presence that commands respect, commands awareness, commands recognition.

He's not home. His car is gone.

I hope he doesn't come back. I hope he stays away. Because as she turns one more time at the top of the steps, looking at me, I know for sure she's mouthing words at me.

Words I've heard before, I realise as a shiver runs up my spine.

My heart aches as I read her lips, the words recognisable even from here.

She slams the door, she and her suitcases gone like she was nothing but an apparition.

This is no apparition, no nightmare this time, though.

Her words were real.

It's all …

I don't know if I pass out or fall asleep, but when I wake

266

up, the words are spinning in my head over and over like a demonic curse.

'Stop it!' I shriek, clutching my head, willing them to stop, willing her to stop.

But I can't. I can never make it stop.

Chapter 41

Three days she's been home. Three long days, three long nights.

Three days' worth of screaming, of shoving, of knives appearing out of nowhere. Three days of watching him cower, watching him beg, watching him fall apart.

She's wearing him down.

I wish the demon had never come back. She should've stayed wherever she was, demented and abusive. She should've stayed gone. It would've been better for all. I know that now. No matter how badly I want it to be untrue, I can't change the facts.

The house was quiet without her, almost serene. There was a calm in 312 Bristol Lane I hadn't seen in a while.

I think he could be happy without her. Maybe she'll go away again.

But there's something different about him, too. Even though she's a tyrannical wrecking ball when she's home, she's also a presence when she's gone. It's like her claws are always in, no matter how far away she is.

It's love. A twisting, demented love built on false hopes and the past. But it's still love. Love doesn't let you choose who gets to dig their claws into you. Love doesn't always give you a choice. Love isn't rational.

And, despite everything, despite her toxic hatred fuelled by rage, he loves her. Despite the pain she causes and the turmoil she wreaks on his life, he adores her. It's sad and it's not smart. I want to shake him, tell him their love story isn't healthy, isn't right. I want to tell him that sometimes love isn't meant to be. Sometimes, two people are just poisonous together.

She's lethal with him, for him.

Still, I sit here, my melancholy attitude making me rock a bit slower as I watch him, sulking at the dining room table, the fifth or sixth beer in his hand. For the past three days, he hasn't left the house, moping around, sitting around, alcohol in his hand at all times.

She's ruined him. She's shattered his confidence, and now, since her leaving, she's crushed him completely. He doesn't know who he is without her. I see that now. Even though with her he's a shell of the man he should be, without her, it's even worse. There's no sense of direction, no peace. Just a crumbled husk of a man she left behind. How could she do this to him? To them? Why couldn't she see what she was doing?

But this morning, as the sun rose, she left again, this time taking the car. No suitcase though. She'll be coming back.

Where is she going? What's going on with her?

I can't begin to understand her.

He stands, staring out the dining room window, long after the car is gone. There's no joy at the sight of her leaving. No joy left at all, in truth.

I haven't seen him smile in weeks. How could I expect him to smile, though?

I stare at him, thinking about walking over there, thinking

about what I should say to him. But what could I say? Who am I to say?

I sit, rocking, pity in my heart for him, an inexplicable love for a man I hardly know.

We sit in this purgatory for a long time, me staring at him, him staring at nothing, blankness filling both our lives.

Emptiness is the thing of destruction, is the start of the downhill descent. I know that now. Maybe I've known it for a while. It feels familiar somehow.

He stands now, leaving the room, walking away. He's gone for a long moment, and I wonder what he's doing. What could he possibly be doing?

He returns, something in his hand, something long. He wipes at his face, looking out the window, studying something. For a moment, my heart stops. I think he's staring at me. Should I wave? Should I stand? Does he see me?

But he doesn't because, after a quick moment, he looks up, up at the ceiling. I don't know what he's staring at.

I feel an icy chill, one I can't explain.

He moves the dining room chair now to a corner of the room, still in view. I don't know what he's reaching for.

What's he doing? She'd be so mad at him for standing on that chair. He's leaving footprints, dirty footprints, all over it. She's going to be so mad at him when she comes home. Is that a rope in his hand?

He's doing something above his head now, the rope dangling. What is he trying to fix now?

I don't understand. I can't think. Something feels terribly wrong, terribly wrong. I put the cat carefully on the floor, standing, my knees cracking as I do. I lean on the window, my hand touching the cold glass as I peer out.

The rope is around his neck now.

Oh, God. No. No. No.

He's pulling it tight.

He isn't. He can't. He won't.

This won't fix it. It's not fixing it. My heart stops. My hand goes to my chest.

Tears start to fly.

I race towards the door, but it's a slow crawl. I need to be faster. I need to do something. I need to stop this. I can't let this happen. This isn't what I wanted, never what I wanted. But when I get to the front door, it's too late. I can see through the big bay window it's too late. He's kicked the chair. His legs are flailing.

I rush back inside. I can make it to the phone. I can get help. I can save this. This can go away.

My heart is fluttering fast, wildly beating. My hands shake, and my legs are like lead. I need to move faster. I need to get to the phone. I need to save him.

It's my job to save him.

I pick up the phone, my fingers trying to find the buttons. It's no use. I stare out the window, seeing his face in a grotesque expression. Terror rips through me as he dangles, swinging. How is that rope holding? What is it tied to? My brain can't process it.

I dial the numbers, numbers I haven't dialled in a long, long time. Numbers I've only dialled a few times. My fingers are clumsy.

I turn from the sight of him swinging, staring instead into my kitchen, the big table sitting where it's always been. I look past the stove, the shiny brass doorknob taunting me. I need to hurry. I need to get in there.

I abandon the phone, tossing it down as I rush across the kitchen, gasping for breath. My hand touches the doorknob, the familiar brass feeling shockingly cold. For a moment, I consider what I'm about to do. I know there will be no going back. A deep dread stirs inside of me. I know that whatever is behind the door will change everything. But I must do what I need to now. There's no time for weakness. I toss the door open into the room I haven't entered in so long.

It's been so long.

But no, it hasn't.

It's happening. I need to stop him.

The door flies open. And there, centred in the bay window, is the familiar, sturdy hook. The hook a plant once hung from. But it also stirs another memory, a much darker one. I realise without a doubt that there was once something besides a plant that hung from that very hook. My stomach drops as it floods right back, the opening of the door opening a door within to the memories I'd rather forget.

That hook on the ceiling looks like the hook I've seen so many times in my memories, in my mind. It looks like the one I've tried endlessly to forget about. Because on that day, when I came home after that final, wretched fight, when I found him dangling, there was oddly one thing I noted. The hook. The hook looked so sturdy, anchoring him to the ceiling. My mind traced the curvature of it, studying it like I was examining fine art. The calmness that settled in as I looked behind the horrors dangling from it struck me as odd, but I couldn't help it. The hook was what I associated with that awful day for decades and decades. It was the reminder I didn't want of what I had done and couldn't undo. Even on that horrific day, my husband's bruised neck and purple face the thing of true nightmares, I couldn't take my eyes from the hook, even when the guttural scream echoed off the walls when I realised I'd finally done it. I'd pushed him too far.

I knew even then that it was my fault. It was completely my fault. The angry words spat at him over our lack of children. The wild accusations every month. The biting words, the degrading monologues, the weapons, and the final straw that afternoon had pushed him over.

The knife to his throat that led to him shoving me down, pinning me against the wall, and threatening to kill me. Ironically, despite all of the times I'd treated him so badly, it had taken me pushing him to violence that had been the final straw. I had gone too far, my rage and darkest desires pushing yet another person I'd loved. I'd destroyed two lives now, and with them, the only hope I had that there was any goodness within me. But still, with all of that swirling in my head, I'd stared at the goddamn hook, wondering how it had held.

The realisations come flooding back at once, the deep truths I've been trying so hard to ignore. I'm trembling with recognition of realities I've tried so hard to shut out. Even after all these years, this room floods me with the sensations I've fought most of my life to overcome.

It can't be. It can't. This isn't happening. It's all a mistake, a horrific nightmare. My hand covers my mouth as I shake my head, staring once again at the hook in the ceiling, wondering how it can hold so much. This isn't true. It hasn't happened. There's no way that it's true.

It isn't though. It isn't. Suddenly, it's apparent. There's still time. There is still time to save him, to undo everything. I know it now. The overwhelming thought terrorises me, and

I freeze. Panic chokes the air in my lungs, freezes the blood in my veins.

The room. It's empty. A dusty old room I haven't been in for years. Not since he took his life that day, leaving me and my moroseness behind ... but is the room empty? Is it too late? I blink, and I can see it all. I see him right here, like I could reach out and grab him. The hook, the rope. The chair. It's all here. I blink again, though, and it's all gone. My brain screams with pain, a throbbing, slicing sensation. I clutch at my head, crying and just wanting it all to stop. Wishing I could stop it. I'm so confused.

One moment, it's like I can see him there, his feet dangling back and forth, back and forth. But then, I look again, and it's just the empty hook, a room that has fallen victim to the stale air of not being used and a layer of dust too thick to swipe away. Back and forth I go, thrown to and fro between reality and the past so quickly, I can't tell them apart. I don't know what's happening anymore.

I take a breath. He's not in here. It's too late.

But no. No, it's not too late. It's definitely not too late, I think. He's not in here. But I can still make this right.

I rush back to my rocking chair, staring out the window, looking out across the yard at 312 Bristol Lane.

There he is! I see him. Silly old woman. Of course he isn't in my dining room. He's over there. He's dangling, his feet kicking wildly. I glance to my right, verifying that the empty dining room in my house is still vacant.

I look back across the street, my head hurting, pounding with confusion. There he is. He's hanging there. He needs help.

How can this be? I grab my head, sure I'm going to die right here.

I want to die right here.

No. No, no no. God, no.

'Amos? Amos, where are you? I need you, Amos. Come over here. Come back,' I yell irrationally. I need the cat. I need someone. I need anyone.

I slump down into the chair, looking back to 312 Bristol Lane. My breath is fast and hard. I can't breathe in enough air.

I can't let this happen. I can't. I'm sorry. I'm so sorry.

I dry heave, tears and snot and the feeling of bile rising in my throat. My head swirls and I see it all too clearly, right in this room.

The swinging feet. The sight of him, my beloved, dangling in the window. I can't stop it. I can't do anything. I'm too late.

I rock back and forth back and forth.

Falling down.

Falling down.

My fair lady.

My fair lady.

Falling.

Fair.

Fault.

It's all my fault. I did this. I pushed him too far. I pushed him, just like I pushed Lucy. It might have been different, Lucy's push a physical one and his a metaphorical shove, but it was still me doing the pushing. *What had I done?*

I take a deep breath, squeezing my eyes shut. And then, deep within, the resolve rises, a resolve I haven't felt for decades.

It's not too late. I have another chance. I can change things.

I stand from my chair, my legs weak but my determination strong. I won't let him do this. I will stop it this time.

I deliberately head for the half-eaten rhubarb pie on the counter, the knife gleaming in the light. I grab the handle, willing my legs to move faster. I breathe in and out, reminding myself to keep moving, to keep breathing. I can stop him. I can save him.

I can save him from himself, but most of all, this time, I can save him from me.

Out the door I go, the screen slamming behind me. I heedlessly rush down the stairs, willing my feet forward, praying I don't fall.

I head towards 312 Bristol Lane to do what I've always needed to do.

When I get to the front door, I grab for the doorknob and fling it back, the knife in my right hand.

I stomp inside the house towards the bay window, hoping I'm not too late. Please God, don't let me be too late this time.

But before I can get to the dining room, before I can figure out how to get him down, how to save him, something puzzling happens, and I squeeze my knife even tighter.

Chapter 42

'Stuart? I have to get to Stuart,' I scream. 'I have to save my husband.'

The man in the doorway doesn't budge. He doesn't move.

'Hello?' he says, looking at me like I'm some ghost. 'What's wrong?' he asks, his face perplexed.

The fear, the sorrow turns to something else now. I feel the rage rising in me, a rage I have only recently felt second-hand through my memories. But now, the rage is fresh. How dare this man stand in my way. *How dare he.* I need to save Stuart. I don't have much time.

Tears well, but I push them down. And, shoving towards the dining room, I see something in the man's eyes I don't like. Something I recognise.

I see pity. I see judgement.

And, before I can see any more, it happens.

The kitchen knife covered in rhubarb pie is covered in something else.

Blood.

The knife pierces the flesh, right through his shirt, and I stare into his face as shock and horror paint themselves on his expression. He moans, a guttural moan of shock and agony, and then he crumples against the wall, slowly sliding down.

I pull the knife back out, blood oozing in patterns magnificent. I stare into his face, calm and collected.

'I need to save Stuart,' I announce, stepping over him, stepping towards the dining room.

But when I get there, I don't see Stuart. There is no noose, no rope.

I don't understand.

Where is he? Why can't I save him? I saw him. Right here. I know I did.

I need to save him this time.

I need to save Stuart. Am I too late? It can't be. I can't be too late. Not again.

Tears whirl, mixed with sorrow and rage.

I just don't understand.

I spin back around, staring at the man who sits in a pool of his own blood. He is sliding away from me, every inch triggering an agonising scream.

'Where is Stuart?' I yell, angering as I trudge towards him.

'Please, don't. Please don't,' he begs, tears on his greying face.

He looks at me with a fear I recognise from another part of my life.

I swipe at my face, shaking my head.

I don't understand. I don't know why I couldn't save him.

I am angry. I am rage-filled. And someone needs to pay.

I step towards him; his eyes are pleading. 'I'm so sorry. I'm sorry, Stuart,' I murmur.

He looks at me like I'm mad.

I'm not mad. I know he's not my husband. I know that.

But I also know he is part of the reason I couldn't stop things. I couldn't save him now.

He got in the way. I was too late. Again. And this time, it was his fault.

The knife throbs in my hand. It begs to be felt, begs to be heard. So I listen.

This time, I look into his face as I plunge it into his stomach again and again. Again and again.

Blood flies. I grow weary.

When I'm done, I grip the knife harder, step over the pool of blood – wouldn't do any good to get my pumps ruined – and head out the door, into the warm March sunshine.

Nobody sees me as I travel across the yard, into the house and back to my rocking chair.

I hold the knife tight as I catch my breath, rocking back and forth, staring at the bay window.

But Stuart isn't there. He never was, I guess. He's been gone too long. It's too late.

And now it's just me again, alone, with Amos by my side.

I rock and rock and rock for what seems like forever.

And then, as I'm staring, I see a truly fantastic sight.

Jane pulls into the driveway, the car roaring into its spot. She's hopping out, shopping bags in hand. I can't believe it. I can't believe my eyes.

She's back. It's too late, though. It's way too late.

She's wearing a sunshine-yellow dress, her short hair still beautiful in the sunlight. She's back. She's home. She's here.

She walks up the driveway, staring into the window as she does.

Nothing to see there, dear. Keep moving.

I watch her walk in through the front door and I wait. I count one-two-three-four.

And as if on cue, a guttural scream escapes from her lips.

I wish I could see her. I imagine she crumples to the ground. I can almost taste her shock from here.

Her scream sends shivers up my spine. I wonder if he can hear it, wherever he is. I wonder if Stuart hears it.

She screams and screams, but no one comes out to help, least of all me.

Because I know I'm screaming now, too. Her screams merge with my own, until they are one. One long, loud scream for the thing we can't fix, no matter how much we want to.

A grating scream for the hook in the ceiling, for the window that looks so different now, and for the woman who was too late.

After a long moment, she rushes outside, and within seconds, there is a pounding at my door.

I squeeze the knife tight. It's too late for Stuart. It's too late for Alex at 312 Bristol Lane.

But it's not too late for her to pay. Someone has to pay for these sins that cannot be undone.

Someone has to pay indeed.

I walk steadfast and sure to the door. I know what I must do. The train can't stop now. It can't.

I open the door, and she's a sobbing, bloody mess. She looks at me and I want to feel pity for her. I want to apologise, to say I understand.

But I don't.

She looks at me as she incoherently mumbles about blood and murder and needing help, but I barely hear her words as I wait for her to rush inside the doorway, until she's right where I want her.

I barely hear her screams as the knife plunges again, its job not quite done.

'It's your fault, it's all your fault,' I say, tears only falling after the deed is done, after the sunshine-yellow dress is bright red.

Because it was her fault. It was the fault of her youth and of her prettiness and of her temper. It was all her fault.

But then again, maybe it wasn't completely. Maybe we are all products of the lives we live, of the circumstances of our earlier days. I can't tell.

With the job done, I toss the knife down with a clatter, head back to the kitchen and pick up the phone.

This time, my fingers find the right buttons. I dial correctly, my voice trembling without any rehearsal.

As I explain the circumstances to the operator, I take one last glance back at 312 Bristol Lane. And then, despite the emergency operator's instructions, I hang up, knowing things will be over soon. I sit down in my chair, staring at the house again, a bit of sadness welling.

Why do all good things have to end so soon?

I rock back and forth, back and forth, back and forth until they come.

There are a whirl of questions. A whirl of answers. A swirling concoction of body bags and police lights and evidence bags. A blanket is thrown over my shoulders and some nice police officer makes me a cup of tea like Jane always did.

His isn't nearly as good. He doesn't know how to make it just right like she did.

And then, after a long time, it's over, just as quickly as it started.

I am alone in my chair, the blackness enveloping me as I drift away, away, away once more.

Chapter 43

Wearing a hot-pink top and tight jeans, the redhead walks hand in hand with her husband behind the realtor. As the realtor in a pantsuit talks about equity and square footage, the redhead pats her bulging belly, glancing at the view from the porch of 312 Bristol Lane.

'And check out this view,' the realtor says, pointing towards the open fields near the lot. 'Isn't it gorgeous? Such a private little lane. Only one other house, and she's just a lonely, sweet widow. No noise, no one to bother you.'

'I don't know,' the redhead says anxiously, looking at her husband. 'I mean, after everything that happened here. It kind of gives me the creeps. Bad vibes and all.'

They walk into the entranceway and the realtor edges them towards the kitchen, talking about cabinets and lighting and floor plans, probably hoping to skirt around the topic at hand.

Murder isn't quite the best selling point, after all.

'Darling, we talked about this,' the husband says, stopping in the middle of the open kitchen. 'You know our budget is tight, and look at this place. A nice backyard, three bedrooms. It's a steal. And you can't even tell anything happened here.'

The woman sighs, her hands instinctively feeling the countertop as she studies the marble pattern.

'But it's creepy. A man was killed here. Right here on the floor. Stabbed to death by his own wife. Doesn't that bother you?'

'Well, I wouldn't say it makes me happy. But come on. These things happen, right?' the husband says, looking to the realtor for help.

In a small town like this, everyone knew everyone's business anyway. But a woman murdering her husband? That was front-page news for a long while. It was still the talk of the town, even though it had been a year.

'The newspaper made her sound like she was so sweet, too,' the redhead says, walking towards the window now. 'Who would've thought she had it in her? All those stab wounds. Crazy, huh? Almost everyone who knew them said they seemed so happy.'

'And then to think she went after the sweet lady next door, too. God, the poor thing must be frightened. And after losing her husband to suicide all those years ago. Honestly, how much suffering can a woman go through?' the husband asks, wrapping his arms around his wife as they look out the window.

'Oh, and look at that beautiful hardwood floor in here, guys,' the realtor says now, still animatedly trying to turn to the conversation to architecture and real estate trends. It wasn't working. The couple basically ignore her, staring out the window. The husband puts his hands around his wife's belly.

'Just think how happy she'll be to see us, a happy new family, raising up our little one here. Poor woman could probably use a friend after all she's been through.'

The redhead stares out, the sun shining down. She puts her hand to the window, her eyes growing misty as if she can

286

see their future, can see all the dinners and movie nights here. She stares out into the yard as if she can see their little one playing catch.

'I heard that the widow's statement to police talked about how the woman here was pretty abusive. That she felt terrible for not speaking out sooner, that she always suspected the woman was dangerous. Sad story, huh? If only someone had known. They could've stopped her.'

'Well, at least she didn't kill the sweet old woman next door. Crazy, isn't it? She was able to wrangle the knife from the younger woman and save herself. Golly, must be some firecracker of an old woman.'

The redhead smiles. 'You know, maybe you're right. Maybe this is the right kind of place for us. I think we could really build a good life here. And who knows, maybe we could help out that sweet old lady next door, bring some joy back into her life. Maybe we could change the reputation of 312 Bristol Lane, bring some positive karma back. You know?'

The realtor tries to keep a poker face, as she reassures the couple of things like market value and resell value.

But in that moment, neither of them hears. The young couple sway in the window, staring at the house next door, imagining all sorts of picture-perfect moments that they will experience in this new stage of life.

And they couldn't be happier, a bright future gleaming in the distance as they make the decision that will change everything.

Epilogue

*T*ap. Tap. Tap.
    Tap. Tap. Tap.

Sometimes in life, it's the simple things that bring joy, that bring meaning.

Like a new cutlery set.

I do miss that old knife I had, but this new one is nice. It's bigger, sturdier. It fits in my hand just right.

Tap. Tap. Tap.

The blade clinks against the windowsill as my chair rocks back and forth, back and forth. I stare out the window, watching the scene unfold, a smile spreading on my face, the knife feeling so cold and so right in my hand.

It's a Thursday when they move into 312 Bristol Lane, a blazing June sun gleaming off the white picket fence as if everything is about to change. Amos jumps into my lap, and I stroke him with my free hand, glancing down only to see the sunlight gleaming off the blade. It's so new and so shiny.

I stare as she pauses from her work, wipes sweat from her brow. Her red hair is tied back in a ponytail, one hand on her bulging belly. I like that she has red hair. It's a nice change.

Despite the excitement, I'm tired this morning. I feel like I ran a marathon actually – ridiculous, since it's been several decades since my feet have run fast. I never was much of a runner, in truth, even in my younger days.

Still, my bones are aching. Did I fall asleep in this chair last night? My back and neck ache like I did. Maybe I did. Who knows. Amos's not telling if I did or not.

I get up to feed him, setting the knife down on my chair before I walk away. I trudge to the bowl, the gloppy food falling on the plate with a squishy sound as the huge cat plods over to his bowl. I decide to make myself a cup of tea and then return to the window, my favourite spot. I slide the knife to the windowsill, just for safekeeping. You never know when the need could arise. After all, you can never be too careful when you're all alone, and some habits die hard.

It's so comforting to see the young couple, so obviously in love. You *have* to be in love to be skipping under the stifling heat, carrying box after box like that. I remember when Stuart and I were in love, so long ago. I remember when I, too, was smiling and happy.

But sometimes things change, I think. Sometimes a woman's true colours shine through, even if no one suspects a thing.

I shove down the memories, the swirling moments of sadness and arguments and of all the hard times. I look at the knife, the new knife, the new start.

I notice the new neighbour's bulging belly. I wonder what the nursery will look like. I wonder if it will be a boy or a girl.

I watch as her husband strolls over to kiss her forehead before unloading another box. He says something to her, motioning towards the steps of the front porch. She shakes her head, but he shakes his, grabbing her arm and pointing to the stairs. She apparently relents, hands in the air, as she smiles, shaking her head and taking a seat. He winks at her, and I smile.

This is what love looks like, love in its truest, purest form, love ready to take on life. I know it.

Staring out that window, though, a feeling of dread creeps in, just a little.

I hope they can make it last, can hang on to the sweet moment. I hope they can find happiness, can find peace.

But an icy panic takes hold of me because, deep down, I know the truth. I know how this ends, even though it's just beginning.

Despite my silent prayers, I get the feeling that before long, the joy will fade, and the couple's dream house will become a prison not much unlike my own.

After all, a woman has a way of knowing these things.

Acknowledgments

First, I want to thank Katie and the entire team at Avon for believing in my story and for giving it a place to call home. I am so fortunate to work with an amazingly supportive, dedicated, and talented team. I feel truly blessed to call myself an Avon author.

Thanks to my husband, Chad, for challenging me to chase my biggest dreams and for supporting me along the way. I am so thankful we met at such a young age. I am so lucky to have you in my corner. I love you so much.

Thanks to my parents for stirring my love for reading and writing at an early age. You have always encouraged me to go after my biggest goals, and I am so lucky to have both of you in my life.

I want to thank all of my family and friends who have supported my writing from the very beginning. Thanks to Tom, Diane, Jamie, Christie, Kristin, Alicia, Kay, Lynette, Ronice, Deborah, Grandma Bonnie, Kelly, and Maureen for being there for me since the beginning of this journey. Thank you also to Audrey Hughey for helping me find my confidence as an author. I couldn't do this without all of you.

A special thank-you goes to Jenny for being one of the first to read and believe in this story. You've been such an amazing friend throughout this process, and I don't know where I'd be without all of our treadmill gossip sessions.

Thank you to all of my readers for taking a chance on a small-town writer with big dreams. I am so grateful to every single one of you.

Last but not least, thanks to my best friend, my mastiff Henry, for showing me what unconditional love looks like and for being right by my side on all of the days I'm writing away.